From the author c
Our Secrets come
for fans o

PRAISE FOR
14 DAYS TO DIE

"This may be called 14 DAYS TO DIE, but it only took me one and
a half days to read it. I was hooked from beginning to end."
—*Sue and her Books*

"Whoa . . . I was not prepared for this. This is a gripping thriller
full of twists and turns."
—*Michelle Only Wants to Read*

"Talk about a fantastic plot and premise for a thriller! Not only
was this one fast-paced, but it also had exceptional character
development . . . Overall a fantastic read that I highly
recommend!"
—*Suspense is thrilling Me*

"I'm pretty hard to please when it comes to psych thrillers
(probably because I read so many of them), so I was pleasantly
surprised by how much I liked this one."
—*Kelly and the Book Boar*

"You will NEVER see the ending coming . . . That ending knocked
me on my behind and left me speechless and ready to scream!
BTW . . . I LOVED THIS ONE BIG TIME!!"
—*Jamie Submits to Books*

IF I HAD TWO LIVES

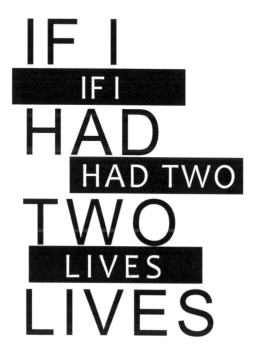

A.B. WHELAN

INMOTION CAPITOL BOOKS – UNITED STATES - 2019

Summary: *Vicky Collins has a seemingly enviable life. She is a successful agent for the FBI and lives with her social media star and real estate entrepreneur boyfriend in an upscale neighborhood of San Diego.*

But appearances can be deceiving.

When Vicky is recruited to an elite unit at the FBI to investigate a serial killer piggybacking on the murders of other serial killers, her life begins to spiral out of control.

To complicate things further for the young special agent, a routine background check at the FBI reveals a sibling DNA match — a brother she didn't know existed.

Determined to unravel the mysteries of her past and to find her long lost brother, Vicky retraces the boy's footsteps through the foster care system, uncovering the abuse and neglect he suffered growing up. The secrets she unveils are more monstrous and terrifying than she ever imagined, and a new truth about her childhood threatens to consume her.

Then the Piggyback Serial Killer strikes again, but this time, Agent Collins has multiple suspects—including members of her own family.

If I Had Two Lives: a novel / A.B. Whelan
    ISBN: 9781699855959
    ISBN 13: **978-1699855959**
        1.   Psychological thriller
        2.   Suspense, Thriller, & Mystery
        3.   Female friendship
        4.   Serial killer
        5.   Sexual abuse
        6.   Family history

IF I

HAD

TWO

LIVES

For those who suffer in silence

"What has violence ever accomplished? What has it ever created?"

—Robert Kennedy

THIRTY-FIVE YEARS AGO

A muffled scream pierced the peaceful silence of the early morning at the nursing facility. Aimee Stone, who at twenty-five years of age was the youngest caretaker at the San Diego Long Term Care Nursing Home, rushed down the hallway. A heinous discovery had been made in one of the patient's rooms, and she immediately went to notify her boss. She allowed herself to walk with the briskness of an eager employee and managed to smile at Kathy, who was heading toward her grandmother's room. Underneath the façade, Aimee's racing heart pumped in her chest, and her churning stomach made her nauseous. But if she wanted to avoid alarming the residents and staff members, she had to get a grip on her emotions.

As Nurse Aimee passed room 132 B, the door slammed against the nickel spring stopper, and Mrs. Horowitz appeared, sullen-faced and frowning, banging her front-wheeled walker against the wall as she emerged from her room.

"Nurse!" she yelled at Aimee, beckoning her. "The negro woman didn't bring my water. I sent her to fetch some over an hour ago. I'm parched, yet nobody cares. What kind of place is this?"

On any other day, Nurse Aimee would gently usher the ninety-three-year-old lady back to her room and calm her down before more racist and other vile things that always upset other patients poured from the mentally ill woman's mouth. When the elderly woman's family admitted her five years ago, they didn't stop apologizing for their mother's behavior, the way she'd insulted everybody. Her adult daughter and two sons went to great lengths to convince the care home's staff of how nice and caring their mother had been to them as children. They blamed her difficult life, bringing up twelve children while struggling with poverty, for her misfunctioning brain. Despite the children's best efforts, they could no longer tolerate their mother's outbursts and decided to seek professional help for her. There wasn't much that the staff of the care facility could do to help her with her mental illness in her old age but to keep her comfortable and isolated as much as possible in her deluxe room.

Today, Aimee had more pressing concerns than to assist Mrs. Horowitz. The secret she had freshly uncovered inside the walls of this very building dwarfed every other matter in the house. The reputation of the facility was on the line.

As the passionate young nurse passed the complaining tenant without acknowledging her, Mrs. Horowitz began to wail in earnest, an accomplishment for the four-foot-ten woman who struggled to simply keep her weight up and move around.

Doors opened left and right along the hallway. Patients poked their heads into the corridor to see the cause of the commotion. Nurse Aimee slipped her hands in her pockets, keeping her eyes on the commercial carpet, then ordered the front desk clerk to call for help as she rounded the corner and rushed across the entrance hall.

Her destination was near. The door to the office of the director (who was also the owner of the business) was only a few yards away. Upon entering the secretary's office, the sight of the vacant chair behind the desk caused the young nurse's pulse to fasten. She could feel her blood beating against the thin skin on her wrists.

Without knocking, she burst into the bright, spacious room of the director's office and found her boss standing by the window, talking on the phone.

The tall man, whose shoulders were as narrow as his hips, spun around and shot an incredulous look through his square glasses at the young nurse. "What in the name—?" he said in his deep baritone voice that Aimee found friendly and pleasing to the ears.

"Please forgive my intrusion, but we have to talk . . . immediately!" the nurse announced, dapping at her damped forehead with her sleeve and pacing nervously.

The director was a friendly man, who was great with people. He knew every employee by name and kept up with their private lives—not in a creepy uncle kind of way but more as an invested mentor. He never forgot a birthday and always inquired about the children of the staff members whenever he saw a picture of a kid pinned to the wall in the nurses' station or the break room. He was a fan of Miami Vice and dressed like Don Johnson. His getup today was a pastel-hued Armani jacket thrown over a tight shirt and matching high-rise pants. He followed football and had an in-house fantasy-football team going with the employees. As a daily routine, the group discussed their teams every morning over a cup of Italian-style coffee made with an imported coffeemaker. Every Fourth of July, the director invited the entire staff to a pool party at his house. The guys would barbeque burgers and the women would watch Dallas on the patio television set in their white skirts and bright summer dresses. Children splashed in the pool and gorged on sweet cigarette-shaped candies (that would be frowned upon today) and popsicles that were never short on supply. Our boss had a permanent smile on his clean-shaven round face, flashing his set of bright white teeth as he patted people's backs appreciatively as they talked. Everybody loved the man and wanted to be him, and he basked in the attention with the flare of a Hollywood actor.

The blunt intrusion by Nurse Aimee didn't invite the usual friendly welcome, though. Instead, the director apologized to the person on the other end of the line and slammed down the phone on the top of a pile of thick files on his hardwood desk. He drew in a deep breath, raised his glasses, and set a pointed glare at the young woman.

Nurse Aimee struggled to find the words to describe what she had seen in the patient's room. She clasped both hands together and swallowed hard. There was no easy way to put it, so she decided that the fastest and least painful way was to quickly rip off the bandage.

"Emma Alexis is pregnant," she announced in a feeble, shaking voice.

The director's shoulders dropped, and his round belly pushed against his pale pink shirt. "What are you talking about? Are you mad?"

Aimee sighed deeply and let out a long warm breath as if that would somehow help clarify her statement. "You know the patient in room 178-A, Emma—"

"I know Emma in 178-A. But what you're saying is utter nonsense! How could she be pregnant? She has been in a vegetative state for years."

"I know. It makes absolutely no sense, but I drew urine from Emma's bag and tested it. The result came back positive. She is pregnant."

It was the director's turn to shake his head. "Sit down!" he ordered the nurse rather harshly—in a tone that was opposite his typical demeanor.

Nurse Aimee put her hand up to indicate otherwise. "I can't. I'm too emotionally disturbed right now. I can't even think."

Mrs. Bourton, the director's secretary, arrived and leaned against the doorframe, her permed bob hair like a helmet perched on her head. "Is everything all right? I stepped out to use the bathroom for a second."

The director waved her away—a gesture that made the ever-cheerful woman shrink a few inches and recoil.

"And shut the door!" the boss shouted after her. She returned a childish pout and pulled the door closed.

"Are you a hundred-percent sure?"

"Yes, I am. I came back from my extended leave today—remember my aunt needed assistance after she broke her hip."

"Yes, yes. I know. I signed your paperwork."

"I was washing down Emma this morning and noticed her usual flat belly was a little round. First, I thought that maybe while I was away, someone had changed her diet, causing her slight bloating. But then I checked her paperwork. She hasn't had her period for four months. I touched her stomach; it was hard. Her breasts too! I checked her recent bloodwork. Her estrogen levels were through the roof. So, I went out to purchase a pregnancy test kit . . . I don't know why I thought her to be pregnant. I mean, she's been here since she was eight and her condition hasn't changed. But I did it anyway. I had this hunch—this bad feeling. I used a syringe to remove some urine from the bag and tested it. I'm no doctor, but she's displaying all the signs of a pregnancy."

As the pale-faced director fell into his plush rotating chair, the printed scoresheets of football games flapped on the wall behind him.

"If this is true, we are ruined," the man said breathlessly. "We are done. Your job. Mine. Everyone in this shithole." His jaws tightened—bones pushing against his tanned skin. "FUCK!" he shouted and swept everything off his desk with his arm.

Nurse Aimee shuddered. "Sir, I could be wrong. We need a doctor to check Emma."

The director leaned back in his chair and propped his hands behind his head. "Let me think for a second."

"With all due respect, sir, this can't be swept under the rug. If Emma is truly pregnant, then there is a predator rapist among us. A man who abused that poor girl is working for you, working with me." She pounded on her chest. "We need to call the police and notify her family."

The director slammed his fists onto the table. "Fuck!" he repeated as if all the available words in the dictionary evaded him. "Look, let's not create any undue panic until we're a hundred percent sure of what we are dealing with here. I want to see her. Gather all her charts and meet me in the patient's room."

"All right, sir. I'll bring them to you."

The nurse reached for the door handle.

"Aimee!" the director called out to her. "Please, not a word to anyone. I'm serious."

The nurse nodded solemnly and stepped out of the office. Without as much as a glance at the secretary, she rushed out to the records room, feeling the piercing eyes on her back. She hated lying and was never good at it. It was difficult for her to remain silent, especially when she knew there was someone in the building who should be cuffed and publicly humiliated for the crime.

She passed Jorge, who used to be a soccer player in Mexico in his prime and now was responsible for the maintenance of the building. Aimee lowered her eyes as her brain was firing with speculation. Although he had an accent, Jorge spoke decent English. He coached a youth soccer team and earned extra cash as a referee on the weekends. Aimee had never noticed him staring awkwardly at any female employees or heard of him making inappropriate comments.

Conversely, there was a part-time psychologist, Tim McGrath. He never missed an opportunity to recite the latest standup comedy jokes in the break room, regardless of how borderline inappropriate they were. There was Scott Adams, the bald male nurse who was obesely overweight, loud, and obnoxious. She couldn't help imagining him wheezing on top of the helpless girl who couldn't move a muscle but still felt everything like any other person. She could feel pain, fear, and hunger but had no power to defend herself. It was painful to consider the ordeal Emma must have gone through.

Aimee's fingers rolled into a ball at the thought of someone violating that innocent girl who was suffering through so much already. She thought of what she would do to the person that committed this atrocity. Rage and fear coiled inside her chest like fighting snakes as she looked for the files in the filing cabinet. The head nurse, Mandee Dee, was in the records room too and put the back of her hand against Aimee's forehead to check if she had a fever.

"I have a slight headache, that's all," Aimee said, without looking up from her search.

"Do you need help? What are you looking for?"

"Emma Alexis's charts . . . Uhm . . . the boss wants to see her feeding schedule."

Apparently surprised, the blood drained from the chief nurse's face. "Why didn't he ask me for the schedule?"

Lies, like bitter pills, sat on Aimee's tongue. "He caught me in the hallway and probably didn't want to bother you with something so . . . so—" She wanted to say "something so basic and irrelevant," but she couldn't bring herself to utter the words, so she shrugged instead. "Got them. All good. See you at lunch."

Aimee tucked the files under her arm and headed to room 178-A. Inside, she found her boss looking down at Emma with a creased face and folded arms.

After a glance at the young woman, nearly ripping her heart in two, she handed the files to her boss and pulled the blanket back to the patient's upper thighs. She pointed to the small bump on her lower abdomen. "See that? I don't think I'm wrong about this."

The director pushed his glasses higher up on the bridge of his nose and immersed himself in reading the files. When he emerged, his face was ashen. "How come nobody noticed the changes in her menstruation cycle?"

"I've only been working here for eighteen months, sir, but I remember she skipped her period a month or two before. We were told it was common for someone in Emma's situation."

"Fuck!" the director blurted out for the third time, causing Emma's heartbeat to elevate. Aimee took note of her pulse on the monitor and leaned in to caress the patient's angelic face while battling to keep back her own tears.

"When was the last time her grandparents visited?" he spoke without making eye contact as if he was ashamed of causing the girl further anxiety.

"I already checked the logbook. The grandparents were here three days ago. They don't visit more than two or three times a year. We need to call them."

"All right. I know someone from school . . . Haven't talked to him in years. He went to med school. If he still practices, I'll get him here to see what he can do to terminate the pregnancy."

"Are you going to call the police and the grandparents?"

"No, not yet. If we can handle this in-house, then we can save the reputation of the business and everybody's job, including yours. Let's get a complete picture of the situation first, then we decide on a course of action."

"What about the rapist?"

"He must be caught. There is no question about it. We can draw blood from the fetus and compare it to our male employees. We have everyone's blood type on file, which is good, as I imagine people won't be willing to give up their blood voluntarily without a valid reason."

"That sounds too risky. We need something less evasive."

"Got any ideas?"

"I'm thinking—" the nurse strained hard to rack her brain for a friendlier and faster solution. "Sir, remember how Emma reacted to your cussing? Her heart started beating faster and her respirations increased. It's how our body reacts to trauma or fear, isn't it?"

"In most cases, yes. Very clever, Aimee." The director pinched his chin, deep in thought. "I'll go and unearth my old school buddy, and you can arrange to have every possible assailant in this room individually and monitor the patient's response."

He no longer called Emma by her name, as if he were trying to detach himself emotionally from the innocent girl who had been the guest of this institute for years.

"How should I do that, sir?"

"I'm sure you'll find some excuse to get people in here. You have three days but no more than three attempts per day. This poor girl must have lived through hell under our watch. If I find out who did this . . . I don't know what I'll do." The director touched the patient's toes through the blanket and then walked out of the room.

* * * * *

The most terrifying and frustrating week followed after the director of the care facility and Nurse Aimee made a pact to find the man who raped and impregnated Emma Alexis while she was in a vegetative state. Aimee went home from work that night, broken and devasted, her faith lost in humanity. She pulled her cardigan tight over her chest, despite the pleasantly warm May weather that evening in North Park, San Diego. Her husband attributed her sadness to the failing health of her aunt. He graciously accepted the reheated leftover dinner of meatloaf and mashed potatoes from the refrigerator. Aimee's grief and confusion strangled her appetite, and she watched her beloved eat as they sat on the sofa in the living room.

The Cosby Show was on, and he pretended to watch it when, in fact, Aimee knew he was focusing on her instead. He offered his wife a beer. Then a second one. She also poured herself a shot of gin in the kitchen and rummaged through the drawers for a pack of cigarettes left from her party days.

The young nurse waited until her husband went to bed before chain-smoking four Pall Malls on the back patio. She was haunted by her vivid imagination, recollecting the possible events Emma had to suffer through under her care.

She pictured the disabled girl in terror as a stranger climbed on top of her, clouding her face with his rancid breath. His sweaty hands groping underneath her nightgown. His drooling mouth latching onto her pristine lips. And then violating her.

Emma must have been awake and aware, feeling every thrust and hearing every groan, lying there helplessly. She had already surrendered control over her body when she suffered a traumatic brain and spinal injury as a little girl. She was in a head-on collision with a drunk driver. Her parents lost their lives in the accident, and young Emma had been living in the care facility ever since. Her brain could sense touch and other sensations but was unable to respond to anything. She couldn't move or talk. She only lay in bed, eyes set on the blank ceiling. Someone so evil—capable of taking advantage of her disability—didn't deserve to live in society.

Aimee leaned against the sliding door and drew in the smell of the city: a hint of the salty ocean, eucalyptus trees, and someone barbequing nearby. The newlyweds were planning on starting a family soon, but how could she bring a child into this mad world?

"Honey, are you coming to bed?" her husband called through the kitchen window, running his hands through his already tangled hair.

"I'm trying. I just . . . I need to see something beautiful to ease my soul."

"Beautiful, you say? Let's see. How about I take off work early tomorrow and take you to the gardens. Mama Grigolato said the flowers are still blooming due to all the rain we had this year."

And just like that, Aimee had a spark of an idea. Emma was staring at the white ceiling above her bed all day, every day. She could offer the idea of painting her room with colorful pictures to please her and stimulate her brain. All male employees would be required to help with this project.

Aimee put out her cigarette, went inside, and draped her arms over her husband's neck. "Did I tell you how much I love you?"

He smirked. "Of course you love me! How could you not love a cool cat like me?"

In the morning, Aimee was up and at it early. Her husband had time to sleep in. The Italian restaurant he managed didn't open for lunch until eleven. Aimee did her best to look as she did on any other day of the week to avoid raising anyone's suspicion.

At the end of the seventh day, she collapsed into the chair next to Emma's bed, drenched in failure. She sincerely believed her plan would work. The concerned nurse had invited every male employee to Room 178-A, but the heartbeat of the young paralyzed girl never increased.

Aimee smoothed her hair back and rubbed her face in irritation, ransacking her brain for a solution. Did I miss someone? Who else had access to her room that would have had enough time to commit such a heinous act without ever being caught?

Aimee put her hand on Emma's hand, promising her to find whoever did this to her.

The director's friend from school had visited two days ago. He confirmed her suspicion. Emma was, indeed, expecting a child.

Despite Aimee's suspicion, the director's childhood buddy turned out to be a sincere doctor. If he was once a drugged-up hippy who got caught up with the wrong crowd in the seventies, he had since cleaned up his act. He was an outdoorsy guy with a mop of dark curly hair and black stubble that dotted most of his face below his eyeline. After his examination of Emma, he offered to bring an ultrasound to the facility to examine the fetus.

The director and Aimee were still awaiting his return.

Aimee's arm reflexively pulled away at the sound of the door creaking behind her. Gus, one of the contractors doing occasional work on the building materialized in the doorframe. He'd come by every couple of months with a crew to remove the leaves and debris from the gutters, clean the glass panels that wrapped around the building, and power wash the tile roof. As usual, his face was swollen and his nose was netted with veins from heavy drinking. A thin, white beard highlighted the ridge of his lower face and stretched up to his ear, giving him the look of Doc from the Seven Dwarfs. He wasn't Aimee's favorite handyman, because he would never look her in the eye, and she didn't trust people who didn't look her in the eye. But he was quiet and caused no problems, so most of the time she hadn't even noticed him.

"Oh . . . I'm sorry to disturb you, babyface. I can come back later," Gus said, pulling back the door with an ashen face and smashing a red bucket against the wood frame. The rhythm of the lulling monotone beeping of the monitor changed, Emma's vitals increasing to the point of alarm.

I shot up from the chair to face the window cleaner. "I was . . . it's okay . . . Come in," Aimee said, eagerly listening to the monitor's beeping. Emma was reacting to something or someone.

The man hesitated, switching his eyes from Emma to the nurse, then stepped inside the room, wearing his signature work coveralls. A bucket swung in his hand, and the cleaning bottles beat against the sides like an orchestra. As he passed the nurse, Aimee caught a whiff of cigarette smoke mixed with cheap aftershave. She had skipped breakfast, and his stench turned her empty stomach.

Aimee glanced at the monitor. Emma's pulse was rapidly beating. Small dark eyes under arched bushy eyebrows of the man were intensely watching her moves.

The stubby man's protruding cheeks were redder now, and there was a sizable pale ring around his eyes.

Fear gripped the nurse, and she froze. The door was only a few feet away from her, and her mind told her to flee, but she couldn't leave this revolting man alone with Emma. In the past week, this was the first time she had showed any reaction to the presence of another human being.

"I think there's been too much excitement for the patient for one day. How about we let her rest and you skip this room this time?" Aimee said, hoping the man didn't notice her trembling knees and weak voice.

The disappointed man looked back at Emma for a brief moment.

"All right, babyface. No problem," Gus agreed trudging toward the nurse.

Alternating cold and hot flashes washed over her body as she escorted him out of the room and forced a smile. She locked Emma's door with shaking fingers, and half-ran, half-stumbled to the director's office.

"I found him, sir!" Aimee blurted, the moment she shut the door behind her. "You . . . you're not going to like it."

The director jumped up, nearly knocking over his high-backed chair. "Well then, who is it?" he asked with an unyielding, anxious expression.

"Sir, it's Gus. Your brother."

EIGHT YEARS AGO

It's a relief to finally reclaim my freedom. The free world is so close I can almost taste it. It's a brutal and lonely world, but it's still my home.

The alarm blares above the door and the barred gate slides open in front of me. I follow the guard to the out-processing station for the final checkout procedure I must endure at the hands of these apes—state employees that walk around with an aura of pride like they own the place; as if they've never slipped up in life. The only difference between them and me is that I got caught.

With every step, the bottom of my pantleg brushes against the top of my feet. I relish the rough touch of the seam of my jeans, the hardness of leather flip-flops cushioning my steps and the softness of my one-hundred-percent cotton tee against my skin. I feel like myself again, minus the stale smell my clothes soaked up while in storage.

I've gained some weight during the past eight months, despite my efforts to regularly work out. I blame the prison food. The company that caters to the inmates uses obscene amounts of salt and sugar to make the otherwise tasteless meals somewhat palatable. We have no right to complain. We are the scum of society.

I close my eyes and summon sweet memories of hot chicken potpies, braised beef sandwiches, and my favorite—the fried sausage and apple dish—served in The Hawk's Head at Riley's Farm in Yucaipa Valley. The first foster family I was placed with after social services removed me from my aunt's care used to take me to that historic farm at the foothill of Oak Glen, treating me to homemade goods and outdoor pioneer games. The head of the household, Rich Ballard, paid ten dollars for me to throw a dozen hatchets into old wood stumps in front of piles of hay. Then his wife, Laura, would take me to pick strawberries in the nearby fields or apples in the orchards.

The Ballards treated me as part of their family, even though their two spoiled daughters, Caroline and Colleen, both my seniors, despised me. They never missed an opportunity to spit vile things at me, to belittle me, or push me around. But I didn't care about those girls because I had my own room and there was food on the table three times a day. A much better situation than my biological aunt had given me when I was dropped into her care after my parents died.

Then my aunt had decided to put down the crack pipe and test clean for the drug screening. She swore to the Riverside County Child Protective Services and to my CASA, my court-appointed special advocate, that she was clean and ready to take on the responsibilities of caring for her deceased brother's son once again. Despite my pleading—begging, crying, kicking, and failed attempts at running away—I was soon back in the house my aunt had bought from *my* inheritance. A mini-mansion is a better word to describe the property. A few hundred thousand dollars bought a lot of square footage in Beaumont, California, but culture and taste didn't come with it.

An army of garden gnomes guarded the front yard, facing the fence in unison like a band of freakish soldiers. The stucco was an ugly pink that reminded me of the girls' clothing section in Walmart—a favorite store for the Ballard girls to fill their wardrobes. The inside of the house was an eyesore. Each space decorated by a spur of the moment inspiration. The inspiration came from anywhere with her. A picture my aunt saw in a magazine, or the design of a doctor's office, or a room decoration at a friend's house. The result was an assortment of bright colors and confused style that would have made my father roll over in his grave.

My aunt attempted to interview a few housekeepers to bring order to the chaos, but one of her coming-and-going boyfriends scolded her for paying for help when she had me. The length and content of my list of chores depended on the parental involvement of the current boyfriend. One passive-aggressive boyfriend required me to mow the yard with the riding lawn mower at eight years old. I might have accidentally run over a few flowers or dinged the shed. My punishment was usually a belt, or electrical cord, to my backside in the garage, with the vengeance of a Viking god. Sometimes, when I was sore and bleeding, I would lie on my bed and cry myself to sleep, wondering if these damned full-grown apes were aware of their strength. Probably not, as they never held back when pounding on my forty-pound frame.

Living with my aunt wasn't all bad. Once in a while, a cool guy shacking up with us would teach me how to be a man instead of cracking down on me for not emptying the dishwasher. Watching the 1980s hit movie *Stand by Me* was bonding time with one role model. We would drink beer and smoke cigarettes like the kids in the film and I learned to cuss like a sailor. As early as fourth grade, I was giving lessons to my fellow students on the most colorful adult language that would leave them in awe.

Those laid-backed dudes never lasted long in a relationship with my aunt. She liked them tough and unpredictable. Structure, quiet, and safety made her restless. Too much of that inevitably led to glass breaking and shoes flying.

As I stand in front of the prisoner-release desk, I notice my neck muscles tightening. All that was a lifetime ago. I'm twenty-five now and too old to dwell on the past. What happened, happened and "it is what it is," as one of my aunt's wise boyfriends used to say. I'm certainly not the first, or last, kid to suffer at the hands of the very people who are supposed to love and protect us.

I scratch the back of my head as I sign for my possessions. Seventy-eight dollars in a faded leather wallet, a lighter, and an iPhone with a cracked screen. The state was kind enough to give me some petty cash, presumably sufficient to buy a bus ticket out of here.

The sliding doors open behind me. Dry, hot air pushes into the room. I steal a whiff of the outside dust and smog before the aggressive air-conditioning unit above the door spewing cold air to keep the obese woman at the desk comfortable halts the scent of freedom. Even the air makes a point to keep us prisoners isolated.

I was sentenced for twelve months to the Larry P. Smith Correctional Facility in Banning, California and required to pay a two thousand dollar fine. I didn't have that kind of money. By the time I turned eighteen, my aunt had pissed away every last cent of my inheritance. I was shy of my sixteenth birthday when we had our last big fight over grades and girls and she kicked me out of the house. If my girlfriend's family hadn't taken me in, I would have been on the streets. Poor bastards, the Sotos, like they needed another hungry mouth to feed.

Once my emancipation was finalized, I started working at a local ranch supply-and-feed store to earn my keep. The money was enough to pay rent for my small, dingy room and rice-and-bean dinners. I had no right to complain because, without the Soto family, I would have been one of those homeless dudes with calluses on their feet and hands layered with grime, pushing around a shopping cart with all my earthly possessions in a plastic bag, stuttering to myself.

For the most part, the Sotos were a decent family; except when the old man, Juan, started to drink. Then all hell typically broke loose. When the storm began to brew, I took off to a nearby abandoned office building to buy drugs from the homeless occupants. It was a three-story concrete frame without walls and windows filled with broken dreams and bad life choices. You had to wade through a sea of tall, dry weeds that scraped your legs bloody to get inside. The grounds around the building had large, random holes and was littered with leftover building materials. At least that dangerous landscape kept the cops away most of the time.

I can't precisely recall when my drug addiction began, but in hindsight, I see that I was heading in that direction soon after my parents left me alone and unprotected in this wretched world.

My father died in front of me, and I let it happen. It was a sizzling hot July afternoon in Encinitas, where we were cooling ourselves at Moonlight Beach. I was trying out my new bodyboard, my father keeping an eye on me nearby when he started gasping for air. He had asthma. One second he was riding the waves next to me, the next he panicked and his body seized up. I watched as the powerful frothy waves of the Pacific Ocean swallowed him up, like some kind of sacrifice to Poseidon. I was right there next to him, but I couldn't find him. I was only six. An age I used as an excuse for years for not saving my father. I still see the look of fright in his eyes in my dreams: "Help me!" they screamed.

Two years later, my mother died of lung cancer. She was a heavy smoker who tried to hide her addiction from us; unsuccessfully, I may add, since an ever-apparent cloud of smoke surrounded her like an invisible bubble. No amount of chewing gum or Listerine strips could mask the rancid smell.

But I loved her. I loved both of them. As an only child, I was bathed in constant attention. If I wanted to try a sport, I only had to snap my fingers. If I craved something, my mother would rush down to the nearest grocery store to get it for me. The walls in our kitchen were covered with my artwork from school, and every participation award I earned was displayed in the living room in a glass vitrine. I was the light of their eyes. I was their everything.

My mother had passed away in a hospice room, alone and scared. I was asleep at home with my babysitter that night. I never forgave myself for not being there with her. Like I needed another reason to brand myself a failure.

After the funeral, my life fell apart. Whenever I lashed out, my aunt tamed my anger with Adderall or Tylenol. By the age of twelve, I was taking painkillers daily, and an extra dose whenever my head hurt, or I felt sad and depressed. I started smoking weed in middle school. In eighth grade, I broke the school record for most suspensions. After that, I never stayed in a town long enough to build a reputation. Courtesy of the foster-family system, I attended three different middle schools.

In high school, drugs were easy to get. Most of my friends had parents who were doped up on anti-depressants or painkillers and who swallowed uppers and downers like they were candy to keep their shit together.

The only way I managed to graduate from high school was by attending summer school, where I was practically pushed through the system.

Life almost worked out for me at age sixteen when I was placed with the Soto family. They genuinely took care of me. I had a roof over my head, food in my belly, and money to burn.

Yet fate had other plans for me.

A woman, ten years my senior, walked into the feed store I worked at on a beautiful sunny morning and offered to buy me dinner for my help. At IHOP, she talked business and flashed a wad of cash. I took it. Two months later, I was the boy-toy to three other friends of hers too. Rich bitches with fat egoistical husbands who had ridiculous money from either working in finance, horse racing, drugs, or human trafficking.

I was only twenty years old when I met her. It took me four years to break free. She wasn't going to let go of her cash cow without a fight. In a heated argument, I punched her in the face and broke her jaw. She played the innocent victim in court, and the judge and jury fell for her act. I was a good-for-nothing hooligan, an orphan, and a destitute criminal. The bitch stole eight more months of my life, that might have been twelve, if not for my early release from prison.

Every time I recall my mistakes of the past ten years, I find myself enveloped in an uncontrollable rage. If I do something stupid again, I could be back in this shithole. I'd do anything to stay out. For eight months, the only colors I saw were cream, blue, and orange, and my most stimulating conversation was about the best brand of tobacco to chew. I needed fresh air and new friends.

As I pocket my stuff and head out, one guard eyes me with suspicion. "You'll be back in less than a year," he says. "I bet on it."

I won't give him the satisfaction.

"Enjoy your day, young man," another stern-faced guard says. "Treat those ladies nice now, ya hear?"

I don't respond because I don't want to waste another minute of my life arguing with these pricks. Some women don't want to be treated nicely. He knows it, and I know it, but neither of us will say it.

I step outside into a pale-blue and cloudless, sweltering July afternoon and pull the pack of letters from my back pocket. I find Jenna's phone number on a handwritten note. I grab my phone. It's dead. I don't know why I expected the guards to return my phone fully charged.

The door opens behind me. "Do you need to call for a ride?"

I refuse to ask for a favor from a man who enjoys breaking down people's pride and humanity.

"I'm good, man," I say, and start walking toward the bus stop.

I ride the bus for almost half an hour to the Walmart Supercenter, where I buy a charger, a bag of chips, and a bottle of real Coke from Mexico.

Once my phone hits ten percent, I call Jenna. She is a fine young woman, who responded to my ad in a Christian paper where I was looking for a soulmate. We've been exchanging letters for five months now. The similarities in our lives connected us. She, like myself, suffered at the hands of others—in her case, her husband's brutality.

"Hey, Boo, what's going on? Did you earn special phone privileges or something?" she woos on the other end of the line.

"I'm out," I say flatly.

While I was in prison, Jenna had shown up for two conjugal visits. I tasted her lips and inhaled the sweet scent of her skin and hair. I was looking forward to a new life with her but had hoped for a few days to gather myself first. But then again, I could only stretch fifty bucks too far. I need money and friends.

She screams, and I pull the phone away from my ear. "I can't believe it. You're out?"

"Yep. I'm out for good."

"Oh, my gosh! I can't believe it!"

"Hey, Jenna. I hate to bother you with this, but I need a place to crash for a bit."

"Of course! Um, where are you now?"

"Sitting on a bench in front of Walmart."

"Okay, I'm gonna get you in ten—no, more like thirty minutes. Don't move, okay? I'll help you get sorted out, my love."

An hour later, I drop onto a bed in a room at America's Best Value Inn for forty-three dollars a night. The motel room oddly resembles the prison. On a rectangular building a row of blue doors with gray windows breaking up the uniformity of the cream-colored walls.

My girl was wearing a flimsy orange sundress, and, once alone, I didn't have to do much to turn her on. She was easily pleased. Her excitement was contagious, and I felt my dark mood lighten. I pulled her onto me and unleashed a year's worth of caged passion onto her body.

Drenched in hot sweat, we lie on our backs watching *America's Got Talent*. The voice of Sharon Osbourne irritates me. First, I don't know why then, I realize she reminds me of my aunt.

Switching the channel isn't an option. Jenna is addicted to this show, and I want to make her happy. I pretend to care about the future of those egotistical, attention-seeking losers singing and dancing on national television because she paid for my room. Also, she is the only person that cares about me for the moment. I've never had a relationship I didn't screw up. So this time, I want it to be different.

When the show is over, Jenna turns to me and kisses my lips. "You know we could have this every day of our lives," she says, peppering my lips with more kisses.

I nod. It does sound good, but I can't allow myself to fall into a world of dreams again. I need to get back on my feet, find work, and rebuild my life.

She gently strokes my face and plays with my hair. "Would you like that? Have me for yourself every day? That's all I dream about. You and me."

I trace the mound of her breast with my finger. "I could get used to it, but what about Brad?"

She props herself up on an elbow and looks into my eyes. "He hurts me, you know? Since I've known you, I've refused to have sex with him. But he takes what he wants. When he wants it. He rapes me if I resist."

I rub the heal of my hand against my forehead. I don't need these images in my head right now. I've served eight months in a correctional facility for being hotheaded. If I slip again, I'm doomed.

"We can't be together while he's around, Boo."

"Why . . . why don't you divorce him?" I stammer. I can't get involved, but rationality doesn't stop my urge to beat that scum to a pulp for what he's done to my girl.

Jenna sits up and pulls her knees to her chest. My reaction wasn't what she was expecting from me.

"You know that's not an option. Brad will never let me go. He'd rather see me dead than with someone else." Her body closes up, and her voice drops an octave.

"Then what do you want me to do?" I ask, regretting it immediately. I can't afford to give her what she wants because that ends with me back in prison. But it's too late. The words slipped out, and she pops the question that will change my life forever.

"I need you to kill him for me—for us—Boo. I will help you."

1

TODAY
SPECIAL AGENT VICKY COLLINS

On the morning of my interview at the FBI's San Diego field office, I wake with a start, drenched in cold sweat, my head buzzing. I tuck my moist hands behind my head and stare into the darkness, enveloped in self-doubt over my decision. Doug is gently snoring next to me—the closest victim to suffer from my mental debate—but ever since I accepted Special Agent Tony Brestler's offer to switch from the police force to the FBI, Doug has become emotionally absent. I needed to talk to someone, just to go over the pros and cons of my new career move one more time, but talking to Doug is as useful as talking to the wall.

Ten years ago, he was encouraging me to follow my dreams to protect and serve over starting a family, even if it meant a demanding schedule. "We are still young. There is so much to do and see in the world. Kids will anchor us down," he would say. Now my demanding job is the fuel to every heated argument we have.

My parents didn't share Doug's view on the benefits of delaying our responsibilities as parents. My mother used to say that schools and our society focus so much on empowering our girls that we completely forget about our boys, and that's why nowadays most of them are such *soft dicks*, scared of commitment.

On my little sister's graduation from the Fire Academy, my father stood rigid, his arms crossed, scratching his chin, as he switched his sight from me (a police officer), to my brother (a website designer) and to my sister in her uniform standing tall among men, and murmured, "This world has gone upside down."

Now five years later, my brother still works on his computer from home, has a wife—who has doubled in size since they had their first kid—and two boys to raise. My sister had become a fire captain in a department full of men. Her face has been all over the local news stations as the media glorified her chief for promoting a female firefighter. They aired little action videos of her running to the truck and pulling the hose, proving for all to see that women can do the same work that men do. What the news didn't show was that the video crew had to shoot half a dozen clips before my sister could get the job done correctly. We still talk about that at every family dinner. Our dad never lets us hear the end of his complaints about why we were so eager to take a man's job. For me, our career choices bind my sister and me together. We both broke up a sausage party at work.

When the alarm goes off, I fling the blanket off me violently enough to wake Doug. We've been dating for ten years, but still not married. Too busy.

He groans and covers his eyes against the brightness of the lamp. "Are you serious?"

"I have to get ready for the interview!" I yell from the bathroom.

He pulls the cover over his head, complaining some more.

Wrapped in a towel, I lay out three carefully selected outfits based on an online image search I've done about female FBI agents.

Doug shakes his head with a mocking smile and gets out of bed.

The pantsuit would make me look very official. The black leather jacket too cool. So, I go with the black slack, white shirt—top three buttons left undone—and a dark-gray jacket.

Before I manage to snatch the right outfit and get dressed, Doug jumps onto the bed, a vape extended in his hand toward me.

"You're gonna mess up my clothes, ass," I frown, pulling the pants from underneath him.

"Here, take a whiff. Helps you calm your nerves."

"Are you out of your mind? You know where I'm going, right?"

"I don't think they will test you on the first day."

"No, thank you. I'm calm."

"Yeah, I can see that." He makes a face, gets back to his feet, and disappears into the kitchen. I take a deep breath and follow him to apologize. It's my big day, yet he's trying to sidetrack me with weed, but somehow, I end up being in the wrong.

I kiss him and say sorry.

He endures my kiss but doesn't reciprocate. "It's okay. I just wanted to help."

Twenty minutes later, I'm in the car, driving to meet the recruiter, Special Agent Gabriel Rose, angry, frustrated, and very, very disappointed.

2

I sit in a chair across the table from Agent Rose, a harassing question clouding my mind. *"Do you think I'm doing the right thing here?"* But I won't ask him that of course. Instead, I sit with my back straight as my mother taught me, making eye contact as I smile.

He seems to be my age, thirty-five-ish. Dark suit and tie. Dark complexions, Greek or Italian genes perhaps. When he smiles at me, his downward-cast eyes shrink, and his cheekbones rise higher. He is a kind of man that would make Doug mad if he found out we spent time together in a room alone, though Rose behaves very professionally, cold even. I don't have the slightest impression that he finds me attractive.

Agent Rose looks down at the questionnaire, a pen pinned between his fingers ending in clean, manicured nails. "Let's go over a couple of things to verify your eligibility, then we can start on the paperwork," he says, pressing the tip of the pen into the paper. "You are thirty-four years old, correct?"

"Yes, sir."

"You have a bachelor's in criminal justice and one in forensic science."

"Yes, sir."

"You are a US citizen and have a valid driver's license."

"Yes, and yes."

"All right, so let's get to the most important question because we already know that you are more than qualified to work for the Bureau. Agent Brestler briefed us on your magnificent work at the San Diego PD. I read the report. Your informant who overdosed on Fentanyl-laced cocaine led J-CODE to make over sixty arrests. The FBI, the DEA, and the US Postal Inspector Police had been working together for over eight months to shut down this Darknet drug-mailing ring, and they sure could use a break. Oh, man, getting the address from a manila envelope from the trash? A magnificent work, detective. You will fit right in here at the Bureau."

"Thank you, sir. You make my involvement sound more significant than it was, but I appreciate the acknowledgment."

He offers me a don't-be-so-modest look, then intertwines his fingers. "So, the only question that remains is this. If my knowledge is correct, you will start with the Cybercrime Unit. However, it is possible that you will be required to travel outside of your area, sometimes even for a longer period as well. Would that cause any problem with your private life? With your plans for starting a family?"

I wonder if they ask the same question to male applicants as well. Suddenly I feel hot, and I squirm in my chair. "I'm not married, sir."

"I'm aware of that. See, it says, *single* here. I'm merely asking this as a friend. See, my father was an FBI agent; we barely saw him growing up. Luckily my mother was there to look after my brother and me, but could you imagine if she was an agent as well?"

I don't answer that because it sounded like a rhetorical question. "Well, yes, I'd like to have children eventually, but it's not in my plans right now."

"Well, the window is closing on you; I mean, you are nearing forty. But don't worry, we have great programs for mothers here at the Bureau."

"It's great to hear, sir. Thank you. But as I said, you don't have to worry about that now. I'm looking forward to working with the FBI. Cybercrime is my specialty. I'm very focused on catching the criminals who hide behind technology, sir."

Agent Rose slams my file shut and claps his hands. "Alrighty, then. You still need to complete a week-long physical training in Quantico and do a few tests. Basic urine and blood tests and a physical, but I don't expect any delay there." He pushes the chair back with his thighs as he stands up and extends his hand to me. "Welcome to the FBI, Special Agent Vicky Collins."

I loved the sound of my new title. Special Agent Vicky Collins. I repeat it in my head as I drive home.

The haunting emptiness of our small house welcomes me. I call Doug to tell him about my interview. He answers his phone, but only to inform me that he can't talk right now. He is having lunch with Ethan from the office.

I hang up and sink deeper into the cushion of the sofa. I can picture Doug perched on a high bar stool at one of San Diego's hip places, taking pictures of his food, of his company, of himself. He will touch up the photos with various apps, smoothing out his skin, reshaping his eyebrows and face. Then he will post the best ones to Instagram with a lengthy caption for his 32,637, and counting, followers who live to see what he had for lunch and to acquire a new piece of his wisdom.

A text comes in: We will be here for another hour if you want to join us. It's your day. Let's celebrate.

No, thank you. I've been subjected enough to eating by myself in my boyfriend's company. Since his success as a realtor came from his increased social-media presence, Doug lives to record every moment of his life. The clothes he wears, the places he visits, the things he does are for the single purpose of being #Instaworthy.

No, having kids with Doug is not in my plans. Sometimes I wonder why I'm even with him. I guess he is my comfort animal to whom I like to cuddle up to when I feel lonely.

No need to celebrate. No biggie. See you later, I text back.

I make a sandwich and gobble it down at the breakfast nook. Then I pack my stuff for my trip to Quantico.

3

The cyber division holds meetings every morning where agents discuss key points and fresh leads in developing cases. We also share information about new technologies to help us penetrate the Darknet and pioneer forensic approaches to tie perpetrators to victims. Criminals take advantage of the continually evolving Darknet and turn most of our investigations into a never-ending game of cat and mouse. The FBI and local law enforcement work together to unravel underground organized rings dealing in child prostitution, sex trafficking, and illicit drugs. Success is hard to come by, but the Bureau manages to catch many *mice*. Yet for every scumbag arrested, ten new ones take his place. This was a job that had no end and brought no glory. From my new colleagues, I learned quickly to learn to live with frustration. I couldn't save Susie, but I was determined to help other children in need.

By the end of my third week at the Bureau, my enthusiasm has begun to ebb. I've caught myself plummeting toward depression from the soul-draining work of searching for missing children online or watching videos of abused young girls and boys being traded by pedophiles.

At the end of the day, I arrive home emotionally drained and physically and mentally exhausted. Scattered around our front yard, palm trees are swaying in the warm summer breeze. I lean back in my seat and turn to look at the empty driveway without Doug's car. Reluctant to spend another night on the couch watching Forensic Files alone, I roll down the windows and turn on my vape. The rush of menthol constricts blood vessels in my brain, and I lean back to enjoy the rush. I put on my AirPods and listen to hardcore punk-rock music on Pandora, transporting me back to college days.

Night has fallen upon me when a set of headlights bathe my car in their bright glow. I toss the vape into the compartment between the two front seats, roll up the windows, and step out of my car to meet Doug.

"Did you just get home?" he asks, loosening his tie as he approaches me.

"Yeah, it was a long day," I lie, although I don't know why. I'm a grown woman. I don't need my boyfriend's permission to smoke. "You were out late," I remark, checking the time on my Fitbit, to shift the focus of the conversation away from me.

"Yeah, I had meetings all afternoon with clients. Later, I grabbed dinner and a few drinks with Ethan. We had to go over our program for the Expo in Irvine this weekend." As he kisses my forehead, I get a whiff of sweet perfume. My jaws clench.

I follow him inside, where I set the Panda's Express takeout on the kitchen counter.

Doug sees the bags and rubs his stomach. "I'm stuffed, baby. Could you put mine in the fridge?"

"You've been very busy lately working such long hours. I guess business is good?"

He props himself up on the barstool, face lit up, eyes shining. "It's unbelievable, babe. My Instagram followers hit 35,000 yesterday, and two more agents joined my team this week. Team Doug now has forty-two agents," he gushes, opening a bottle of expensive scotch for his glass with perfectly square ice cubes and a personalized coaster with his picture and realtor information.

"That's fantastic, honey. I'm very proud of you," I say, listening to the buzz of the microwave heating up my dinner.

Doug spends the next ten to fifteen minutes taking pictures of his evening nightcap, then the same amount of time composing a post to accompany his image.

When I reenter the kitchen, showered and in my bathrobe, he looks at me dumbfounded, checking the time.

"Wow, that was fast, babe." He slips his phone in his pocket and stands up. "I'm gonna rinse off too."

I put away the bottle of scotch and drop the ice into the sink. *What a poser!*

It takes Doug another hour to come to bed.

"Maybe we could go on that camping trip you've been talking about," I tell him.

He is clearly amused by something he sees on his phone. "I won't have a free weekend for a while. Ethan and I are taking our presentation on the road. Almost every weekend we'll be in a new state. Most of our events are already sold out," he informs me while speed-typing on the screen.

"Oh, all right. Maybe some other time then, huh?" Less than a year ago, the boys were traveling to be in the audience of presentations given by millionaire realtors. Doug's business barely survived the first five years; he hardly had any listings and spent heavily on educating himself about the trade. If not for my cop's salary to support him and his partner, Ethan, who Doug met in class while getting his realtor license, through the hard times, he would have had to find a stable paying job. I didn't expect a thank you, but a little bit of gratitude would be nice now that he is a success.

To lessen the awkwardness of being ignored, I read for a while, then I switch off my bedside lamp and roll to my side to keep my eyes away from the light of his cellphone, shining onto his narcissistic face, as he responds to comments and counts his likes.

I don't blame Doug for our slowly deteriorating relationship. If I had chosen to be a teacher or the like, then I might have been able to be a mother of two or three children by now, going to baseball games and dance recitals. But my fate was sealed at the age of six when my favorite cousin was kidnapped right under my nose.

I still remember that day like it was yesterday. My father has been working as a traveling salesman for a medical equipment manufacturing company as long as I can remember. When he was a young father, he was gone most of the days during the week, visiting hospitals as far as Northern California, Utah, Nevada, and Arizona. Every summer, he would take a three-week vacation, and we would spend it in a cabin with a private beach at Bass Lake, near Yosemite National Park, with three other families. My mother's older sister, her husband, and their daughter, Susie, and my father's two younger brothers. The youngest, Steven, was only seventeen at the time. The second youngest, Mike, was twenty-seven years old and had a new baby with his wife. We all got along very well.

The night of Susie's disappearance, my father and his brothers were sitting around the fire by the lakeshore, playing cards and drinking. An otherwise mellow and hardworking man, who had dedicated his life to his family, my father could transform into a raging monster whenever he looked at the bottom of the bottle. My mother was no saint, but she always foresaw the trouble brewing on such occasions and would send us kids to our rooms. We would heatedly protest because staying up late on a warm summer night to play hide-and-seek was our favorite pastime.

Susie had asked me to go with her to her room, but I was too angry and frustrated about how the night turned out to be in a mood for company. I'd decided to sleep in my own bed and go to sleep as fast as possible, so I could wake up early to start the next day fishing off the dock.

Under the veil of the night, Susie was taken from her bed.

I heard nothing.

I saw nothing.

The local media and police shadowed us for the following week of our vacation. I remember the lights, the noise, the chaos. I didn't understand what was happening. Why would someone take Susie?

My mother tried to shield us from the truth, so I grew up without knowing all the details about my cousin's disappearance. When I joined the force, the first file I dug up and examined was Susie's.

I learned that the local law enforcement and hundreds of volunteers had combed the nearby woods and divers searched the lake with no results for days. On the sixth day of her disappearance, hikers found Susie's body in a shallow grave, covered with loose dirt and leaves. It was a hot and humid summer that year, and her body was already showing signs of advanced decomposition, making the investigators' job that more difficult. The pictures taken at the crime scene still haunt me to this day.

There was a bite mark on her right shoulder. The forensic odontologist took dental impressions from my father and uncles. He matched the bite to Steven's mold. My teenaged uncle was dragged away in cuffs, cameras flashing in his face.

Steven denied his involvement in Susie's kidnapping and murder. He loved her, he said, and would never dream of hurting her. There were no other DNA samples collected from her body for comparison.

My father hired a big-shot lawyer, who requested a second opinion on the bite mark. The evidence was sent to the East Coast to a highly esteemed video specialist, Dr. James Klein. He enhanced the image of the bruises left by someone's teeth, with a revolutionary new software NASA had developed, and discovered a small gap between two molars that may have been caused by a chipped tooth, ultimately excluding Steven as a suspect.

The investigation dragged on for over a year and a half. Although the perpetrator was never found, the media managed to ruin our family's reputation. My friends no longer came over for sleepovers or playtime at our house. Our birthday parties and holidays were celebrated at home without any extended family. It was as if we had all lost faith in one another.

I would watch other kids with envy as they received hugs and gifts from relatives at school promotions or after soccer games, while my family never came. My heart grew callused after high school. I still wonder what direction my life might have taken if I only went with Susie to her room that night.

4

I enter the conference room with a cup of coffee in my hand. Some agents are already sitting around the table, their hot beverages steaming in front of them. The room smells like a cesspool of bad morning breath.

Agent Brestler rushes in and scans his eyes over the group until they land on me. "Agent Collins, come with me," he calls out to me in a somber yet somewhat excited tone.

My stomach shrinks. Did I do something wrong?

I make my way to the glass door and feel my colleagues' eyes on me as I follow the man who first invited me to the FBI down the corridor and into his office.

Both chairs in front of Agent Brestler's desk are occupied. A woman with smooth ebony skin sits in one of them. She looks younger than me and is dressed in an elegant navy-blue pantsuit. The other chair supports an overweight man in his late forties whose pale hair shows signs of balding as he leans on the backrest with both hands.

"This is Special Agent Collins who works with the cyber unit," Brestler hurriedly introduces me as we make our way to his side of the desk.

"This is Special Agent Anaya Reed from our field office in Las Vegas. She is from the other side of the pond, but once we snatched her up at Berkley twelve years ago, she never looked back, right?" Brestler winks at the female agent. "And Special Agent Bob Henson from Salt Lake City," he finishes up the introduction.

They both acknowledge me with a simple nod.

"Let me start by noting that everything we discuss here today is highly confidential," announces Brestler, making a point of locking eyes with me. "The media cannot, I repeat, *cannot* get wind of this."

I feel my entire body tense up. When was I ever suspected of leaking sensitive information to the media? Doug sometimes asks me about my work, but I only share bits and pieces with him about cases that really get to me. I've never gone into details or disclosed names and locations. Doug could find out more about recent cybercrimes with a simple Google search than with what I tell him.

All three of them look at me for confirmation.

"Yes, sir, I understand."

Brestler pulls out a chair for me then takes his seat behind the desk. "Agent Reed, please proceed."

The female agent leans forward on her chair and addresses me in a British accent. "Two days ago, with the phenomenal work of the Las Vegas forensic team and the local sheriff's office, the FBI apprehended a man who we believe is responsible for the deaths of five young women in Las Vegas. The victims were sexually assaulted, strangled, then dumped naked in the back streets off the Strip. The same MO was used in all five murders, and we've been looking for almost two years for the serial killer with very little success. There wasn't much evidence to go on, and despite our efforts to catch that Bearded Vulture, all five cases went cold."

I catch Agent Henson rolling his eyes at the unusual name. Bearded Vulture?

"Then, we caught a break," Reed continues. "The Las Vegas forensics team managed to isolate a partial fingerprint on the fourth victim's body. They also found fibers that connected the victims. Well, I don't want to go into details at this point, but with the new evidence and some luck, we arrested a suspect. A forty-two-year-old man named Gary Froelich. In his home, we found other vital trace evidence and an extensive collection of incriminating items. When presented with the overwhelming evidence, Froelich confessed to all the killings, except one. Froelich denies any involvement in the brutal death of the third victim, Sarah Duhamel. As you may imagine, his statement raised a few eyebrows with the Bureau."

Agent Reed pauses to clear her throat and takes a sip of what appears to be hot tea with milk.

"Should I be taking notes?" I ask Brestler, but he tells me it's not necessary.

"Everything that's being disclosed here is in the files." He points to a mountain of paperwork towering on his desk.

Agent Reed sets her steel glance at me. "So, what do you think, Agent Collins, why should we concern ourselves with the words of a serial killer?"

"I don't know. Maybe there's a copycat killer out there who sort of 'piggybacks' on other crimes?"

Agent Henson smiles as he gives a glance of satisfaction to Brestler.

"Exactly," says Reed. "That was our conclusion. Someone is trying to pin a murder on a killer at large. We have recently gone over the evidence with a fresh set of eyes and looked into the timeline of the murders. It turns out that there were typically three to four months between Froelich's homicides, but the third victim, the one Froelich insisted he had nothing to do with, happened only two weeks after the second murder. Sixteen days to be exact."

"Did you find any other evidence to suggest another suspect?"

"No, we did not. However, sometimes, the lack of evidence tells us more than the evidence itself. Forensics compared the pieces of fiber found on the four victims, which they eventually matched to the carpet in the trunk of Froelich's car. The Duhamel girl had no fibers on her." Agent Reed lifts up a box of assorted cookies from the desk and extend it toward me. "Biscuits?"

To not to come off as rude, I take one.

Henson turns to Reed. "May I?"

"Please."

"Sarah Duhamel grew up in Santa Clara, Utah," Henson begins, wheezing slightly. "It's a small town about ten miles from St. George. She just turned nineteen when she took a bus to Las Vegas to pursue her dream of being a dancer. Soon after she arrived in Vegas, she was kidnapped and brutally murdered. Nothing about her as a victim stands out when compared to the other four victims."

"You can study the case files and draw your own conclusion," interrupts Reed.

Henson shakes his head vehemently and wipes the sweat from his mustache. "All there. Every detail. I'm just trying to get to the point here."

Reed forces a smile and crosses her legs.

"Only the absence of carpet fibers and the words of a serial killer separates Duhamel from the other four victims," Henson concludes hastily. "Agent Reed and I put our heads together and looked at a few other unsolved murders in the Nevada and Utah areas. There was one promising lead, but we suspect there will be more. As you can imagine, the amount of data is enormous."

"I can imagine, sir," I say, feeling excited. I sense an offer here. "How do I fit into the picture?"

"Agent Brestler told us about your excellent work in data processing and your keen eye for detail. We could use someone like you to help us comb through the hundreds of unsolved murders in California, Nevada, Arizona, and Utah."

"That's a wide net to cast," I say, envisioning myself growing old in front of a computer screen.

Henson pours himself a glass of water. "The Bureau has authorized us six months to compare murder cases in those four states. If we find anything tangible, then we get more time and resources."

"Who's on the team?"

Reed smiles. "You're looking at them."

"All right. Which office will we be working from?"

Reed gives a sly smile. "I'm single and Henson's divorced with no kids. We understand that you are engaged and Brestler has a family here, so we will use the San Diego office as a base to accommodate you two."

I'm not engaged, but I don't correct their assumption. I barely spend any time with Doug as it is and taking a work assignment in another state would surely be the last nail in the coffin for our relationship.

"All right. I'm in. When do we start?"

Agent Reed pops up and approaches me. "Great! Welcome to the team. We'll meet for our first briefing on Monday morning at eight."

We all shake hands. Brestler then shoves the mountain of files into my arms. "A little light reading for you this weekend," he says before ushering me out of his office.

5

Three months into our classified investigations, Agents Reed, Henson, Brestler, and I have identified eight murder cases with suspicious circumstances where either the suspect in custody denied his involvement with one specific victim's death, or in two cases the murders were still unsolved.

We have been working in a spacious and bright office on the fifth floor, overlooking Vista Sorrento Parkway with its small bleak hills and untended lands marking the horizon.

The furnishing of the room was straightforward. Pinboards secured to the white walls display a complex net of pictures, notes, and newspaper clippings. In the center of the room, a rectangular table was laden with files, paperwork, and laptops.

The investigation has been a tedious job of constant reading, researching, data analyzing, and brainstorming. Sometimes I daydream, gazing at the sunbathed streets outside and wishing I was at the beach, living another life. But what we are doing is damn important work.

There is also an upside to being confined to the office: we are allowed to drop the suits and wear more comfortable attire in the office—khakis and a standard FBI polo shirt, though Doug said I looked like a college boy in that getup.

Brestler was offering us fresh pastries and coffee from a local French bakery he brought in to celebrate our success when Henson bursts into the office, ambushing us with a stern face and sharp expression, flanked by two keen agents I recognize from around the office.

"Agent Collins, please step away from the computer!" Henson calls out, arm extended toward me, gesturing me to follow him.

His detached demeanor and cold tone shoot a ripple of shock through me as if a dozen razor blades have been released in my chest.

I swallow the bite of chocolate croissant in my mouth and put down my coffee.

"What's going on?" I ask, pushing away from my desk.

"I need you to come with us. You'll be briefed soon."

Brestler steps forward and places a hand on Henson's shoulder. "Bob, what's going on here?"

Henson shrugs off Brestler's hand. "All work is hereby suspended until further notice. Gentlemen," he instructs his companions, "collect Agent Collins's computer." They squeeze past him in their suits and ties, moving with purpose.

The colleague, with whom I went to the Beer Garden last week when our team grabbed a drink after work, leads me into an interrogation room. He would drink with us, but it wasn't a secret that his conservative ass has never accepted Anaya and me as his equal. I'm aware he'd be happy to see either of us fall.

"You're scaring me, Bob. Have I done something wrong?" I ask, sitting down on the chair I'm offered.

"Please address me as Agent Henson during this interview." His lips stretch, but it's not a smile that comforts me.

The door opens behind me and Tim Ellis, Special Agent in Charge of the FBI's San Diego office, steps into the room.

I don't know Ellis well. He, unlike my old boss back in the PD, never joins his agents in the break room for coffee or shares his thoughts on sporting events. All I know about him is from office gossip or the Facebook search I conducted on him before I joined the Bureau.

The chief is a former Marine who walks with a straight posture, bursting with confidence. He starts his mornings with an hour kayaking in the harbor and ends his days with Krav Maga. He is married to his high-school sweetheart, and they have two girls in high school and one in college.

He puts a laptop on the table and props his butt on the edge. "I'm sorry about the theatricals, Agent Collins, but in special circumstances like this, we must follow protocol to the tee. Today, at 1008 hours, your DNA profile was entered into the Federal DNA Database, as well as CODIS. A routine follow-up procedure for all of our agents."

"I-it had to come back clean," I stutter, doubting my entire being.

Ellis pats my shoulder and turns to open his laptop. "Indeed. However, our DNA analyst found a similar profile to yours in CODIS. A male relative of yours that you had failed to mention on your paperwork.

Consequently, his name didn't pop up when we did our background check on you. Based on the similarities in your genes, we suspect he's your brother. So forgive me if I'm a little suspicious about your failure to mention him." *Seriously, that's it? Then what was all the theatrics about? Oh, lord, Henson must have loved humiliating me.*

Then as the words sink in shock presses me against the back of my chair. "I don't understand, sir. You are telling me that I have a *what*? A brother I don't know about?"

Ellis purses his lips and straightens up. "According to the DNA analyst's report, yes. See, the problem we are facing here is that we suspect you failed to mention him on your paperwork because he has a criminal record."

A million thoughts violently swirl in my head, making me dizzy. "Sir, I know I've only been working for the FBI for a few months, but you must believe me when I say that I have no idea what you are talking about. A brother? Who? Where does he live? What's in his criminal record?"

Ellis glances at the screen of his laptop. "He did some time in the Larry Smith Correctional Facility in Banning for assault on a woman about eight years ago. Then nothing. He falls off the face of the earth."

I prop my elbows up on the table and drop my head into my hands. Then I rub my face with my hands and smooth my hair back to refresh myself, so I'm able to comprehend what I'm hearing.

"I don't understand what's going on. I need to talk to my parents. May I see his profile?"

Ellis turns the screen toward me, and I see a picture of a young man with a thick head of hair. His handsome features buried underneath an uncared-for, tired and bruised layer of skin. But his eyes cut deep into my soul. "I've never seen this man in my life," I announce with confidence.

I don't look up from the screen, but from the corner of my eye, I see Ellis and Henson communicating in silence.

A series of knocks on the door is followed by Reed's dramatic entrance. "Chief. Henson. Whatever you think Agent Collins did, she didn't do it. We've been working side by side every day for months; she is an excellent and dedicated agent. She goes above and beyond to fulfill her duties—"

"It's okay, Anaya. It's just a misunderstanding," I interrupt her, closing the screen of the laptop.

A wave of relief washes over her face. "Oh! Chief?"

"All good here, Agent Reed. You may return to your station," Ellis orders.

Reed puts a hand on her heart and exhales loudly as she looks back at me. "You red-breasted sapsucker! You scared the crap out of me!"

Anaya is an avid birdwatcher who tends to call people the most exotic and strangest bird names. Her cubicle is postered with pictures of wild Alaska. Her dream is to see the great gathering of bald eagles for the salmon rush. When she showed me YouTube videos of that spectacular event, I wanted to go there too. After those dehumanizing days in the office, spending time in the pristine wilderness, far away from civilization, started to sound very appealing to me.

"Henson, you too," the chief ordered the fat man. I now loathed him for being so eager to bust me for something I didn't do. I was glad to notice the registered shock on his face at Ellis' words.

"Chief, I'll take a polygraph test if you want, but you must believe me, I've never seen this man. I grew up with my brother, James, and my sister, Heather. I still don't understand how this man, this criminal, is my real brother. I can't imagine my dad cheating on my mom, but I also don't live in a dream world, I understand it could happen. My dad did often travel for work and would usually be gone for days at a time. If he somehow had another family in another state or city, my mom would probably have never known about it. But what you are saying means—"

I turn away because the mere thought of his statement hurts me. I thought I knew my parents. But forensic evidence doesn't lie; people do.

"Agent Collins." The chief's voice draws my attention to him. "I'm sure you understand that we, as the Bureau, need to investigate this. Lying on an application or withholding the truth is a serious offense with discipline up to and including termination. Now, I do believe you. That's not the problem. However, we still need to untangle this mess."

"I understand, sir. If it's true that I have another brother, I need to find him too." I utter the words between clenched teeth.

"How about you take a few days of paid administrative leave to sort things out on your end. In the meantime, we will wrap up our little investigation here."

My face burns with shame. "Yes, sir. I'll do that."

Halfway to the door, Chief Ellis steps in front of me to partially block my path. "I really do hope this clears up fast, Collins. You've been doing a hell of a job for the Bureau, and I'd hate to lose you."

"Thank you, sir." I bob my head and step into the hallway, tears pushing against my eyes.

6

Leaning against the door and holding my head with one hand, I'm waiting for my mother to answer the door. After studying all the information on my mystery brother and driven by a feeling of betrayal, I drove to Temecula—a rapidly growing city an hour's drive north of San Diego—to find more answers. My parents moved up here about four years ago after my mother took a head nursing position at a local nursing facility for the elderly.

The heat radiating from the concrete patio underneath my feet is slowly enveloping me in an uncomfortable bubble, increasing my aggravation. Coming home to visit is something I typically enjoy. Now, though, I'm rattled and unhinged.

I look at the fish in the wine barrel by the front door, swimming to the surface for food at the sight of me. Bees buzz and land near the water, coming for a drink on this hot afternoon. I think with fond memories of my dad's fresh honey with butter on warm toast; he harvests the honey from a single hive he cherishes. I rub my face to dismiss the memory because I feel blindsided and lied to, and I won't leave until I find out the truth.

I go around back because nobody answers the door to let me in. I find my mother hunched between two rose bushes in the backyard by the pool.

"Mom!" I call out to her.

Startled, she falls back onto the yellowing lawn. "Oh! Jeez, Victoria, you scared the life out of me!"

"What are you doing?"

"What do you think? I'm pruning the roses."

The slow warm breeze brings a whiff of cigarette smoke to my nose. I don't react to it, though I always wondered why Mom never got rid of that nasty habit. Now I know; her dirty secret was driving her on.

She peeks at her watch. "Why aren't you at work, sweetheart?"

"I need to speak to you."

"Well, then let's go inside. It's like purgatory out here. I'll fix you a strawberry lemonade."

We go into the kitchen where it's nice and cold, the air conditioning buzzing rhythmically. I sit down on my childhood chair—old furniture that feels so alien yet familiar to me. Mom's cat crawls onto my lap. As my fingers dig into her soft fur, I begin with a blunt question. "Mom, did you have another child apart from the three of us?"

The bag of frozen strawberries drops from her hands and onto the counter. I help her pick up the runaway berries.

"Oh, thank you, honey. I'm so clumsy these days," Mom chuckles softly.

I cut the lemon and squeeze the juice into the Nutribullet I bought her for Christmas. She adds the frozen berries, sugar and water. I wait until the mixer stops and ask her again. "Did you and Dad have a kid before me?"

She smiles. It comes off more like a grimace, her hands shaking. "Of course, we didn't. You would have known if we had, wouldn't you? Now, what is this silly inquisition all about anyways?"

I put down the knife and lean against the cabinet. "The Bureau checked my DNA profile against their database—it's a routine procedure—and they found a match. They say he is my bother."

Mom's eyes enlarge at my statement, but she doesn't seem to be as interested in this development as I am. "It has to be a coincidence, honey. I have three children. I did not have another before you."

I watch my mom's skin, awaiting the pearls of sweat to appear. I take her hands into mine and place my thumbs on her veins to check her pulse on the sly. She is disturbed by my question, but she appears to be telling the truth. Although I'm not a lie detector.

I drop her hands and turn away. "This whole thing doesn't make any sense." I bite down on my lip and look back at her. She is pouring the lemonade into two tall glasses. "Was Dad ever unfaithful?"

She smashes the pitcher onto the counter, spilling red liquid onto the cream-colored tile. "Never! You hear me, young lady?" She points her index finger at me. "Your father is a decent man. He lives for this family."

"He was gone a lot," I push, hoping to chase her into a slip of the tongue.

"Yes, he was gone a lot—working. He sacrificed his life so you could have a happy childhood void of pain and sorrow." Her lips quiver as she eyes me with utter disappointment.

"What pain and sorrow are you talking about?"

Mom touches her face, then her hand slips down over her heart. "Victoria, I need you to leave. I'm not feeling well and need to lie down. This heat gets to me." She fans her face with her hands.

"Are you alright, Mom? I didn't mean to excite you."

"No, no, honey, it's the heat. Truly."

She walks me to the door. "You need to push this silly idea from your head. They made a mistake at the FBI, or it has to be a coincidence. You three are my only children. If your father did have some bastard out there, I'm sure I would have found some regular unexplained large withdrawals from our bank to support them. Which I didn't."

"Will you ask him for me?"

The tone of mom's skin darkens with a rush of blood to her face and chest. "No, Victoria. I will not. He is always exhausted when he comes home from a long trip nowadays. I will not bother him with this nonsense."

"Where is he now?"

"He's up, as usual, in St. George, Utah for the first week of the month."

I catch a glance of a framed picture behind her on the wall, a photo of my mother and father posing at the beach. They were a young, beautiful couple in their early twenties, full of love and life. They were the kind of attractive couple whose presence must have drawn adoring and envious eyes. I wondered how many advances by other men and women they both were tempted with during their thirty-six years of marriage.

That train of thoughts makes me wonder if any of those temptations ever led to an affair. If they did, they would never tell me. But this isn't some random case I'm obliged to investigate. This suspicious craziness has put my job on the line. If my parents have a secret, I intend to find it, though I've never been so scared in my life to find a skeleton in a closet.

7

I arrive at the Larry P. Smith Correctional Facility at 18:05, hungry, thirsty, and in desperate need of a quick bathroom stop. Tumbleweeds spin across the mostly vacant public parking lot next to me as I roll up to the gate. I flash my Special Agent ID to the guard to gain access. After a short examination, he instructs me to park by the visitor's entrance. An armed correctional officer waits for me to get out of the car. The warm, dry air presses against me, and my skirt and silk blouse cling to my body immediately. Doug would be pleased to see me dressed-up once again, but I would love to change back into my office uniform.

The asphalt feels soft underneath my feet as if melting from the heat. My walk is stiff from driving three hours as I follow the tall, round-faced man with a chubby chin into the building. I'm asked to wait for a word from the warden and told that it may take a while since it's after business hours.

In the waiting area, I help myself to a bag of chips and a pack of chocolate-chip cookies from a vending machine before refreshing myself in the restroom.

Good news waits for me at the front desk when I return. The warden left at five for the day, but his deputy is ready to see me.

I surrender my firearm and empty my pockets before I pass through the metal detector. The deputy warden is meeting me in the hallway leading to the cafeteria. He is a friendly man who maintains a close relationship with the inmates, the escorting officer informs me.

The knocking sound of my heels echoes down the long corridor and announces my arrival. The deputy has plenty of time to inspect me before I reach him, as do I. He is a short, well-dressed man with close-cropped light hair that's thinning at the crown.

My presence induces a round of catcalls from the dining inmates. The deputy nods at his officers to restore order. Avoiding eye contact with the prisoners, I extend my hand to the deputy.

"Vicky Collins, FBI, special operations," I introduce myself.

"Matt Zielinski, Deputy Warden."

"Thank you for seeing me on such short notice," I start, clenching the tablet to my chest. "I understand my visit seems rather unusual, but if we could talk in private, I'll explain why I'm here."

Zielinski laughs and pushes his glasses up higher on the bridge of his nose. "In my line of work, Agent Collins, I'm afraid I'm seldom surprised."

I nod with a courteous half-baked smile.

The deputy puts his hand on my back, indicating me to get moving. "I'm very proud of this establishment. We have one of the lowest rates of lawsuits against us in the county. Plenty of exercise options, well-balanced meals, and a wide variety of educational classes are offered to the inmates to keep them content and busy."

I'm happy to hear that murderers and rapists are enjoying a well-balanced life, financed by taxpayers and their victims' families.

"Sounds like management is doing a great job," I comment.

We turn right at the corner. The greasy food smell fades into an odor of antiseptic and stale water.

"Well, we do the best we can with the budget we have. The elected officials and the inmates' lawyers watch us like hawks, waiting for us to slip up so they can pounce on us. We have to be magicians trying to keep the wheels spinning."

I smile and shake my head. "I can only imagine. I'm hoping your record-keeping is as excellent as your operations." I leave my thought dangling. Zielinski offers me a curious look as he ushers me into his office.

"So, what can I do for you, Agent Collins?" He gestures for me to sit down. "As you may know, we don't get many visitors from the FBI, so I'm curious to hear what do I owe the pleasure?"

Zielinski's chair is set higher than mine, as he noticeably looks down at me. He places his small hands on his desk and crosses his short stubby fingers.

"I came from the San Diego field office to acquire information about a former inmate of this establishment released eight years ago."

"You can access every inmate's file from the comfort of your office. Why drive up here?"

"Yes, I can access some," I turn on my iPad and show the criminal profile to the deputy warden. He pulls his glasses down and glances at the screen. His blank expression tells me he doesn't recognize the face or the name.

"What more do you need?" He leans back and starts gently rocking back and forth in his chair.

"I was hoping to talk to the guards who worked his block. A roommate, perhaps."

Zielinski unfolds his arms and clears his throat. "Let me see what I can pull up on him."

He revives the screen of his desk computer. "Name?"

"Blake Sullivan."

"Date of Birth?"

"September 29, 1985." This must be a fake date or a mix-up because I was born on November 2 in the same year. The DNA analysis must take another look at the profiles. However, this birthday doesn't exclude the possibility of my dad fathering a bastard around the same time I was conceived. I'll need DNA samples from both of my parents to compare.

Zielinski claps his hands. "Here he is. Served eight months out of twelve. Sentenced for physical assault, causing bodily harm to a woman. Released on good behavior. According to his record, he was a model citizen under our roof." Zielinski peers over his screen at me. "We have excellent programs for rehabilitating criminals. Of course, they don't always work, but in Sullivan's case, the results speak for themselves." He pauses as if anticipating a compliment.

I offer him the praise he's seeking to keep myself in his good grace before I ask, "Are you able to track down a roommate or a guard who might have known him?"

"Let's see. Sullivan was in . . . Housing Unit 14. Had two cellmates during his stay with us. Let me see if I can pull up info on them."

I wait impatiently. My right leg is twitching. It's surreal that I have a felon for a brother I've never met. A stranger who crossed the law and lost. A criminal. I wonder whether I'd be able to recognize him on the street. A man can change for the worse in prison. Did he get back on his feet or is he living on the street? Is he a drug addict? A flood of painful questions washes over me as I sigh. Why would my parents lie about something so significant?

"Ah, here! You're lucky. Mr. Paul Gooden is our guest once again. Wow! His rap sheet is as long as the Colorado River. Battery. Assault. Burglary. Grand theft auto . . . I, uhm, I guess he's good at everything but covering his tracks," he snorts with a chuckle.

"Is it possible for me to interview him?"

Zielinski checks the time on his watch. "After dinner. I don't see why not."

"Perfect. Thank you so much. You've been more than helpful, sir."

The deputy blushes. So, I pepper him with more praise to keep him going before I announce my next request.

"Did you find any guards who might have known Sullivan?"

"To go over the schedules to see who worked in that housing unit, that specific year will take more time." He taps his desk with the back of an elegant black pen. "May I ask, why are you interested in our former guest?"

"Of course. He's a person of interest in an ongoing investigation being conducted by the FBI. I'm afraid that's all I'm allowed to disclose at this time."

"Very well." He shrugs and lifts a red mug to his lips. "May I offer you something to drink?"

I lay my tablet on my lap. "A cup of coffee would be fantastic."

Zielinski presses a button on the intercom on his desk. "Denise, would you please be so kind and bring in some coffee for Agent Collins and myself?" he nods at me. "Sugar, milk, creamer?"

"All three, if I may."

He raises his brows and recites my request to his secretary.

8

The interview room is a sterile rectangular space furnished with a white plastic table and two chairs. The remnants of the dying sunlight penetrate the barred window and warm my hands. Behind me, an armed guard stands motionless. His bony face is severe and stern.

Nearly thirty minutes pass before Paul Gooden is escorted inside the room and ordered to take a seat opposite of me. As he sits down, I open my jacket and free the top two buttons of my blouse.

Gooden is a charismatic, handsome man with smooth dark skin and alluring eyes and a single teardrop tattoo under his right eye—not what I expected the criminal to look like. He smiles at me flirtatiously, creating a dimple on each of his cheeks. I wonder why such a good-looking young man would commit all those crimes to end up here, wasting his life behind bars. He could have achieved anything with that face and body.

"Ma'am," he addresses me politely.

I feel hot inside, worried about showing my rookie bones at a professional interrogation.

"Mr. Gooden," I return his smile. "Were you told why I wanted to see you?"

He shakes his head. "Nope. The guards only said that some hotshot FBI agent is here to ask me some questions."

I turn on my iPad and pull up Blake's mug shot. "All right. Do you recognize this man?"

Gooden presses his manicured index finger onto the screen, spins the tablet toward him, and leans forward for a short peek. "Maybe."

"He was your roommate in 2011."

"It's possible." He places his elbows on the table, and now our faces are so close I can sense his warm breath. I don't lean away. He is not in charge, I tell myself: I am.

"What can you tell me about him?"

He raises his brows. "I didn't say I know him."

I run my tongue over my upper teeth, then smack my lips. "I don't have time to play games with you. I have the power to make your life easier . . . or less so in this wonderful facility. It's up to you which one it'll be."

"Are you threatening me, Agent—" he waits for me to finish his sentence, but I won't give him that satisfaction.

I tap aggressively on the screen. "Did this man ever talk about his plans once he got out?"

"Maybe. Maybe not."

I open my mouth, but before I utter a sound, he chokes the word in me. "Uh-uh. Careful now with your threats. I got a lawyer who will take good care of me in case I suffer any kind of abuse in this shithole."

I pull back my tablet and push myself to my feet. "My mistake. I was going to offer you some commissary credit and an extra thirty minutes of fresh air every day, but I guess I'll find someone else who has the information I need."

Gooden grabs ahold of my wrist. The guard leaps toward the inmate, but he releases me swiftly and tosses his hands in the air. "I was joking! Lighten up, people. Yeah, I know him. Blake. Cool dude."

"I'm okay. Thank you," I tell the guard.

"If you open your blouse up a bit and show me some skin, I'll tell you everything you want to know." Gooden winks and licks his lips.

I feel ashamed using my sexuality to extract information out of this man. I've spent my entire career trying to blend in with the guys, to be looked at as an officer, a detective, an agent, and not as a woman. But I am a woman, so why not use that to my advantage? I move my chair, so the guard behind me doesn't catch me releasing a few more buttons on my blouse. If my father saw me now, he'd call me a hypocrite. "You are only a feminist when it suits you. You aren't so eager to do a man's job when it comes to landscaping or washing the car, are you?"

"Nice!" Gooden remarks, rubbing his chin.

If we met in a bar, I'd have a drink with him. That's how vulnerable I feel. The wolf can hide in sheep's clothing, and I would never know the difference until it was too late.

"Ok, you got what you wanted, now let's hear what I want."

He chuckles, folding his arms over his chest. "I'm sorry. He didn't tell me anything. On the day of his release, he got up, said bye, and walked out the door."

Enraged and embarrassed, I button up my blouse, gather my stuff, and get up. The inmate's leering eyes follow my movements.

"I'm done here," I tell the guard. As I make my way around the table, I duck to Gooden's ear. "Too bad you weren't more helpful. I was about to arrange a private room for us to have some fun," I whisper and brush my fingers along his jawline.

"Wait!" Gooden yells after me. "I just remembered something!"

I step out of the room without faltering.

9

Sitting in my parked car in the vacant lot outside of the correctional facility, I open the folder on my lap that the deputy warden left for me at the front desk. Sheets of freshly printed paper slide out. I lift the top page and carefully read through it.

As it turns out, I already have most of the information in my possession. I searched the databases at the Bureau before I left the building to commence my forced vacation, but I flick through these pages, all the same, hoping to discover any new significant facts about Blake Sullivan's life.

"The deputy left this file for you; it contains everything we have on the inmate you are investigating," the desk officer said as I rushed out of my interview with Gooden.

I asked her about the 2011 guard shift schedule, but it wasn't ready yet. I left my phone number and email address to be contacted as soon as it was available. I went back to my car, not an iota smarter than I was when I arrived.

Sitting behind the wheel of my car and balancing the paperwork makes me feel confined. I'm also tired and hungry. The combination of discomfort and frustration brings the grumpiness out of me. Luckily, no one is around to suffer the wrath of my unpleasant mood.

I slide the seat all the way back and roll down my window to release the hot, humid air stuck in the car. I search the compartments for a snack but only find a pack of chewing gum. I reluctantly pop one into my mouth, knowing it will only jumpstart the acid production in my stomach and make me hungrier.

When the first draft of breeze cools my face, I return my focus to locating my alleged brother.

The profile picture in the file is the same one the FBI has listed in AFIS and CODIS: a sunken-faced, pale young man with pimples and bloody scratches on his cheeks. He has a nice shaped head topped with an unruly mop of dirty-blond hair. Blake is giving a cocky grimace in the photo. His Adam's apple is bulging underneath the skin of his neck as he keeps his head back, staring defiantly into the camera. He must have been high or drunk when this photo was taken as his eyes are glazed over.

I trace my fingers along his jawline and park my fingertip by his eye. I try to feel some connection to this stranger, but it's nothing there.

Despite his hard appearance, it's difficult to picture him breaking a woman's jaw. In the file, the guards and therapists only sing his praises. It appears Blake was a well-liked fellow at Smith's.

His record is squeaky clean—suspiciously so. In my experience as a detective, a man capable of inflicting such violence on others, especially on a woman, is hardly a model citizen and has prior offenses. Blake had none.

Next, I look at his personal history. His residences only date back ten years.

He was emancipated from his legal guardian at the age of sixteen. After that, he had only one address in Hemet, California. His primary emergency contact info has the same address. The name listed with it is Juan Soto.

I pull up the address on my Google Maps app. It's a thirty-minute drive from here. If I left now, I could be there by 20:30. An inappropriate time to visit a working family on a Tuesday night.

I'm a long way from home, so I consider getting a room in Banning and visiting the Soto residence tomorrow, but I'm worried about what Doug might think of me staying out all night.

Speaking of the devil, my phone rings. Doug's name appears on the screen.

"Hey, babe," I answer, with a lump in my throat. I don't know why I'm always nervous about telling my boyfriend that I have work to do. He, of all people, should understand my situation: he is in realtor mode twenty-four/seven. He lives for his clients and social-media followers, not thinking twice about sacrificing our private life for the benefit of his business. My memories of the old Doug have long faded away. Sometimes I feel I don't even know the man I'm with anymore.

"Where are you? It's eight o'clock," he asks impatiently.

"I'm out on assignment. I meant to call you but was caught up in an interrogation."

"Out where? I thought your detective days were behind you?" I hear his car door open and a rhythmical warning signal chime in the background.

"Well, when we decided I would join the FBI, we both knew I wouldn't be buried in an office every day."

"Whatever you say, but you could have called me. I have friends waiting for us at the pub for a drink. I came home to pick you up."

"What's the occasion?"

"Since when do we need a reason to go out? Damn, Vicky, you're turning into an old hag."

I draw in a deep breath to keep my emotions at bay. "I'm sorry for ruining your plans. I would go home if I could, but I think I'm going to stay here overnight. I'm over a hundred miles away, and I don't want to risk driving in the dark when I'm tired."

"Where are you?"

"Banning."

"What the hell are you doing in that shithole?"

"Following a lead that turned out to be a dead end."

A sigh echoes. "No worries. I'll make up an excuse for you then."

I feel downtrodden again. A drink with friends sounded much more fun than sleeping tucked between bleached sheets in a sketchily cleaned motel room.

"Doug. Look, I'm sorry for missing this, okay? Why don't you get the gang together at our house for the Fourth of July? We could throw something on the barbeque, make a few cocktails, and watch the fireworks."

"You mean, I could throw something on the barbeque?"

"Well, then hire a caterer. You work with them all the time. We don't have to deal with the food."

"Let me ask around. Are you coming home tomorrow?"

The sound of his car engine starting up drowns out his voice.

"I should be, but I'll call you anyway to let you know."

"Take care of yourself, alright? Love ya," he says this last part with no affection in his voice, like an afterthought or out of habit.

"Yeah, love you too."

After I hang up, I google for any available nearby hotel rooms. Prior to Doug's call, I was leaning toward a cheap motel for the night, but now I feel the need for something a bit more extravagant.

I book a king room at Morongo Casino and Resort with a desert-canyon view and roll out of the parking lot. The spa closed at seven, so I missed any chance of a deep tissue massage, but the bar and pool are still open.

During check-in, I keep reminding myself that Doug and I haven't had a real vacation in ages and I deserve a night of relaxation, but guilt completely takes over by the time I get to my room.

A couple of mini-bottles of wine stacked in the room's refrigerator rejuvenate my adventurous spirit, however. I shower and head down to the buffet to eat.

As I enjoy a slice of medium-rare prime rib with mashed potatoes and corn on the cob, I delve into the files once again.

Blake's secondary emergency contact listed in his paperwork is a woman named Barbara Sullivan. The relationship and the address aren't identified, only a phone number with a 951 area code. I make a note to call her, hoping she might be able to tell me more about Blake's whereabouts.

Blake Sullivan had no transgressions prior to the assault. After I read through the description of his uneventful life in prison, my expectations of finding anything of value fall to zero.

I flip the file closed and head to the dessert bar. I wonder what the hell I'm doing conducting an unauthorized search for a missing brother I've never known. But it's too late to stop digging now, especially when so much is at stake. I have to find Blake Sullivan and prove to the chief that, if he is indeed my blood brother, then it was a secret kept from me by my parents and not a stain on my family's reputation I intentionally tried to hide.

When I return to my table with a plate of various dessert samples, I check Doug's Instagram to see if he's posted about the gathering at the bar. He never disappoints. An enhanced colored photo loads on the screen, showing his highly touched up and altered face that makes his jawline look narrower and his face more defined. He is sitting by the bar, posing between Ethan and a blonde female, his arms looped over their shoulders. The caption reads: *You are the average of the five people you spend your time with. I'm lucky to be working with these two insanely smart and hardworking friends of mine.* Dozens of hashtags follow: *#entrepreneur #boss #agent #businessman #success #workhardplayhard*, etc. I stop reading through the list before I throw up in my mouth.

He never posts a picture of me or us. I guess having an FBI-agent partner isn't as *cool* as working with a young and sexy mortgage lender.

I poke at my cup of tapioca pudding, my appetite drifting away. People laugh around me, enjoying a late-night dinner with friends or family. I'm the only one sitting at a table alone.

To escape the exposure of my sad little life, I gather my belongings and head back to my room. I change into a bathing suit I picked up at the gift shop on the first floor and go back down to the pool.

I smuggle a pocketful of mini hard-alcohol bottles into the hot tub, where I lie back, letting the buzz envelop me and numb my racing brain. The strong scent of chlorine is nauseating, and, mixed with the booze, I soon drop into a dream world.

I open my eyes at the sounds of water splashing. A man, a few years my junior, is in the hot tub with me. His elbows are resting over the edge, his eyes set on me.

I sit up straight and push my back against the jets, embarrassed.

"Sorry, I didn't mean to startle you," he says, smiling.

He is not particularly handsome for my taste, but there is a mischievous look in his eyes that I find alluring. He reminds me of the boys' soccer coach from when I was in high school. I spent endless nights talking about that coach with my girlfriends during sleepovers; about the things we would do to him and would let him do to us.

"It's all right. I better get going. I'm getting prune fingers anyway." I turn my hands palm out to show him my creased skin. "I'll let you enjoy your privacy." As I push up from my sitting position, I falter a bit. In a heartbeat, the man scoops me up and steadies me. I avoid his eyes as I sit upon the ledge.

"I think it's better if you take a breather before leaving. You don't want to hurt yourself on your way back to your room."

I chuckle idiotically. "That would be embarrassing."

"Happens to the best of us. It's quite dangerous being in a hot tub by yourself. I know someone whose husband drowned in a hot tub while using it alone."

It's a strange feeling to allow myself to talk to a stranger under these conditions. It's an even stranger feeling to admit to myself that I yearn for company. Doug is out tonight, drinking and having fun with his female associates. If I questioned him about it, he'd say there's no harm in talking.

I learn that my companion's name is Tyler. He is twenty-eight years old. The company he works for installs fire-suppression systems and he is at the casino for a maintenance issue. He lives in Calabasas. None of those details matter to me because he is funny and exciting, but the detective in me can't stop interrogating him. He doesn't seem to mind sharing his personal information with a woman he just met in a hotel's hot tub.

We order a few cocktails to keep the party going. I'm aware that I'm not supposed to get too friendly with a stranger when drinking alone. Not to mention that I have a boyfriend who lives with me, and I was raised better than to forget that.

Tyler pulls out an electric vape from his bag, and we take hits from the device like college buddies. I laugh so hard that my side hurts.

It must be getting quite late, but I don't want to go back to my cold and empty room. Most likely Doug is still out too.

Now that I've learned my parents have been lying to me my entire life, I feel abandoned. It doesn't help that since joining the force years ago, my childhood friends and I have slowly drifted apart too. Now I have no one left to trust.

Lethargy takes over my mood. Tyler moves close to me. His wet naked upper body is steaming in the night air. I lean back against the tiles. Tyler puts his hands on my waist, and I let him. His fingers trail down to my knees. He separates my legs and pushes into their cradle. He starts kissing my neck.

"It's okay if I do this?" he asks in a mere whisper, hypnotizing me with his dark eyes.

I scream NO inside, but I'm too enthralled to move or say a word. Not because I'm afraid of this stranger, but because I want this man close to me, I want him to touch me, even though I know it's wrong.

He pulls me back into the hot bubbling water and onto his lap, gently kissing me. His hands go on a discovery tour of my body. The sensation of being wanted and desired numbs my senses. He slips a finger inside me, and we go a step further into adultery. Then the edge of the hot tub scraps my back and the pain shocks me back to my senses.

I push away from the young man. "I can't do this. I'm sorry."

He looks up at me with puppy eyes. "Did I hurt you?"

I bury my face in my hand. "No, I-I gotta go."

I step out of the pool and wrap myself in a towel, picking up the empty bottles in haste.

"I shouldn't have pushed myself on you. I'm sorry."

I stop for a second and gather my thoughts. I look Tyler in the eye and clear my throat. "You didn't do anything wrong. I live with someone. I shouldn't have—" the last word dangles in my mouth; the sentence unfinished. "It was nice to meet you, Tyler. I hope you enjoy the rest of your stay," I say before rushing out of the pool area and back to my room.

I pace back and forth in front of my bed for some time, time that seems an eternity, restless from the romantic episode. On an impulse, I get dressed and go down to the casino where I gamble away nearly five hundred dollars on slot machines in an hour.

10

The alarm finds me tangled in the bedsheet and drenched in sweat. The six-hour sleep I managed to squeeze in last night wasn't nearly enough to cure my hangover. My head is killing me, and I'm in desperate need of a cup of strong coffee and solid food.

"Damn it, you're never going to grow up!" I lecture myself as I crawl out of bed to take a cold shower.

My hair is dripping water onto my naked shoulders when I call reception for the clothes I sent down last night for laundry. I'm tempted to order room service and skip the free breakfast, but spending almost a thousand dollars on this night-out to spite Doug makes me think twice. He'll call to question me about the money when he checks our joint bank account. He always does. I'll tell him that the Bureau will reimburse me for the expenses, which usually diffuses the situation.

Dressed in yesterday's clothes—although washed and steamed—I step into line to get some scrambled eggs, roasted potatoes, an English muffin, and some fresh fruit. The coffee is thin and tasteless, so I pour myself three cups to feel a jolt of caffeine.

"Good morning," a familiar voice floats over my shoulder, startling me enough to spill a bit of coffee onto my eggs. "Oh, sorry, let me get you another plate," says Tyler, reaching for my food.

I snatch the edge of the plate to prevent him from taking it. "It's fine. Don't worry about it," I say without making eye contact.

"How'd you sleep?" The manifestation of my shame pulls out a chair at my table and sits down across from me. He waves down the server for coffee and orange juice.

"Probably as good as you did," he says jokingly to ease my discomfort.

I'm not in the mood for sharing breakfast with a stranger who had his finger in my private parts a few hours ago.

"How long are you staying in the hotel?" Compared to me, Tyler seems incredibly calm. His surfer t-shirt is wrinkle-free. His hair is styled and glossy. He must have spent a decent amount of time in the bathroom to look that good this early in the morning.

"Actually, I'm about to leave. Duty calls. I-I mean I have to get back to work," I stutter, crossing my utensils over my half-finished food and finishing my water.

Tyler's face drops and his eyes darken. "Too bad. I was hoping we might spend some time together today."

I briefly glance at him, then pull some cash from my wallet to leave a tip for the server. "Yeah, taking a day off to have some fun does sound nice, but you know how it is."

I'm trying to be nice, but I feel I'm only encouraging his advances toward me, and I can't deal with this right now. I have to call the Sotos and drive to Hemet to talk to them about my missing brother. I need to clear my name and get back to the vital work I've been doing with the team.

I get up from the table and offer my hand to Tyler. He shakes it with a blank face I can't read.

"It was nice meeting you."

"You too," he says.

From my room, I call the phone number listed in Sullivan's records as a contact number for Juan Soto. A woman answers in Spanish. I introduce myself, and in return, she hangs up on me. Astounded, I redial the number. The phone rings and rings until the same woman answers in English this time.

Once again, I tell her my name and that I'm from the FBI. She asks me what I want with her. After I tell her it's about Blake Sullivan, she agrees to meet me at the location that's listed on the paperwork.

Armed with a sense of accomplishment, I check out at the front desk and walk to my car in the parking lot. My stride slows when I notice Tyler leaning against the driver's door of my car. His arms are folded over his chest and his legs crossed as if him knowing my car was a natural thing.

I elect to approach him with a stern statement to lay down boundaries. I may have been misleading him with my kindness, but this is going too far. "Look, Tyler, I appreciate the attention, and I'm sorry if I gave you the wrong impression, but this has got to stop."

"Wow!" he raises his eyebrows as he pushes away from my car. "That's not the Vicky I met last night in the hot tub."

I'm getting a bad vibe from this guy. My instinct tells me to draw my gun. I feel its weight on my side, holstered underneath my blazer. I play a few steps ahead in my head to ready myself.

"You're right. That was the alcohol talking. But like I told you, I have a boyfriend. In fact, we are about to get married," which is not true, but I want my relationship to sound serious enough to deter him, "so what happened last night was a mistake."

He inches toward me, standing tall and dominating. He is a good head taller than me, which I didn't notice last night while sitting in the bubbling hot water.

I sweep my eyes from side to side for witnesses, but we seem to be alone unless there are people behind me.

He gestures with his hand at me. "Come on, Vicky. We had fun last night. Why stop there? What happens in Morongo, stays in Morongo, right?" He laughs.

My patience is wearing thin. How many times do I have to tell this guy I'm not interested in him? "All right, big boy! I gotta go. Find someone else to play with."

I pop the car door open and reach for the handle. A rookie mistake. Tyler slips behind me and pins me against the car door with his hips. "I'm so sick of you bitches always using alcohol and drugs as an excuse for your slutty behavior," he sneers into my ear, so close I can feel his warm breath on my skin.

Within a fraction of a second, I pull my Glock from the holster underneath my jacket and press the barrel hard into his neck. "Back off!"

He quickly staggers away from me, and while pointing the gun at him with one hand, I push open my blazer and flash my FBI identification badge tucked inside my blazer at him.

He quickly ducks between two cars and disappears from my sight. I search the area for him with the tip of my gun, millions of thoughts running through my head. This predator should be arrested before he hurts someone—if he hasn't done so already. I catch the back of his light-pink shirt dashing across the sea of cars. I could shoot him—I'm a good shot.

I lower the gun in my hand and holster it. With my heart hammering in my chest, I take a big breath and look around to find somebody who may have seen us. An older couple is dragging luggage a good hundred yards away from me. They argue as they tread on, oblivious to my presence.

I should go back to the hotel and collect information on my assailant. But if I do, Doug will likely find out about last night. "Stupid! Stupid! Stupid!" I bang my head against the car.

A greasy palm print with visible fingerprints on my window catches my eye. Driven by shame for my lack of professionalism, I remove my makeup bag from my purse and brush the prints on the window with dark eye shadow powder. I lift the fingerprints with pieces of clear tape and set them on one of the documents I received from Smith's.

The ridges and details of the prints are clear and visible. I place the evidence carefully into a bag I find in the glove compartment. I'll be looking up Tyler in AFIS when I get back to San Diego. If that's even his real name.

I spend a bit more time sitting in my car. The right thing to do would be to call the local cops or at least conduct a preliminary investigation on my own. My instincts tell me to settle with the fingerprints for now. That despicable human being was confident enough to approach me and pin me to my car in broad daylight. I'd bet he has other registered offenses. He won't get away. I'll catch the bastard soon enough.

11

I call Doug from the car on my way to Hemet to see the Sotos. It's a little past nine in the morning, but Doug's voice is chirpy and alert.

"What time did you get in last night?" I talk to the speaker as I make my exit from Interstate 10 to Highway 79.

"I don't remember. Not that late. How was your night?" Doug says, gasping for air.

"Why are you breathing so hard? What are you doing?"

I hear the familiar sound of weights thudding onto the hardwood floor.

"Working out. I won't have time to hit the gym today. I have to prep Angela for the open houses this weekend."

"Okay," I remark, dismissing the fact that my boyfriend often works with attractive and smart women. "Did you ask your friends about the Fourth of July party?"

"Yep. We're good to go. What time will you be back?" Doug asks between gulping down some drink.

"I'm on my way to interview a witness about a case I'm working on, then I'll be heading home. I'll pick up burgers and sausages for the barbeque and see you at home around four-ish?"

"Wow! You are cutting it close. You do know that the house needs to be cleaned, right? I want to remind you that inviting people over was your idea."

I stab at the horn before I answer, to alert a man on a wobbly bicycle swerving in the middle of the lane. "Freaking idiot!" I blurt out, navigating around the shabby-looking guy, who is either drunk or high.

"What's going on? You okay?" There is actually concern resonating in Doug's voice.

"Yeah, I'm okay. This place is a whole other California, I can tell you that. I don't know how people can live like this."

"Are you alone?"

"Yes, I'm alone. Why?"

"Aren't agents supposed to travel in pairs?"

"I'm alone in the car, but I work with a team," I lie.

"Any Chris Hemsworth look-a-like man-in-black hitting on you?"

"Don't be ridiculous."

"Jeez, Vicky, take a joke! Well, I gotta bounce. See ya later. Don't forget to pick up a few cases of 805 too."

Doug disconnects the line without giving me a chance to tell him that I find his jealousy flattering. I'm just a little too unhinged today to appreciate it. Maybe it's better I didn't tell him. Doug is so conceited he'd never believe I'd cheat on him and his feigned jealousy is no more than a meaningless statement.

* * * * *

As I approach my destination, the air begins to reek of manure. Soon, I find the origin of the stench: dairy farms and horse properties. These parts of southern California are strikingly different from the track homes and manicured life where I live. It's good to get out of my bubble sometimes and broaden my perspective; it makes me a better investigator. I actually enjoy getting out of the office and doing fieldwork. If only the circumstances were different—

Following the instructions of the GPS, I turn into a trailer park and move along the quiet streets. It's too warm to be outside, and as the day moves on, it will be hot enough to test the endurance of even the most hardcore southern Californians.

I pull over in front of a single-story manufactured home with a sea of rocks for a front yard. Two rectangular windows dominate the façade of the small house. The poison-green blinds are pulled down, but the gate hangs open. Uniform and clean, the house blends in with the rest of the homes in the neighborhood. There is nothing here that strikes me as unusual or suspicious.

For I moment, I wonder whether this was the home my brother grew up in. Once I step inside, will I be faced with photographs of his childhood, trophies of his achievements, and clues about his failures? Studying his bedroom might give me a better understanding of his personality. I may even uncover the reason behind him becoming a criminal. Children act out where they feel the safest. In an ideal world, a family home should be the place where kids can blow off steam, so they have more patience to follow social norms in the outside world. My brother was imprisoned for the physical assault of a woman. Based on the science of psychology, we know that children mostly act on learned behavior. They mimic those around them—primarily parents or guardians. Oh, God, I hope Juan Soto isn't a wife beater.

I approach the front door and press the button on the Ring brand doorbell. In the absence of footsteps or any kind of noise from inside to indicate someone is coming to answer the door, I show my ID to the camera on the Ring panel.

I stand uneasily, knowing that someone is watching me on their phone. I'm about to ring for a second time when a voice addresses me from behind. A short and lean Hispanic male with a shovel in his hand stands by the lone Mexican palm tree that ornaments the porch. "Can I help you?"

Holding my ID out, I face him. "Yes, I'm Special Agent Vicky Collins from the FBI. I made an appointment with Mrs. Soto earlier today. I'm here to talk about Blake Sullivan."

The man lets out a long sigh and leans the garden tool against the house. "Come inside. It's cooler there."

12

The inside of the Sotos' house is as clean and organized as the outside. Plain eggshell-colored walls, thin white baseboards, beige carpet, and a patch of light linoleum with tile motifs in the kitchen.

The man who introduced himself as Juan Soto leads me to the sitting area. On my way to the sofa, I study the dozens of framed pictures hanging on the walls and perched on shelves. The photos are of baptisms, weddings, and birthday parties. By the time I reach the living room, I have a pretty clear picture of the Soto family. There's Mom, Dad, and three girls. But no photos of Blake Sullivan.

Juan yells over his shoulder toward the back room, and the Spanish chatter abruptly stops, as if someone turned off the television.

A short woman in jean shorts and a t-shirt that stretches over her barrel upper body emerges from the hallway. She approaches me with an annoyed expression. Her warm, slimy fingers slip out of my hand as she meagerly introduces herself as Rosalita. She sits down on the farthest spot on the couch from me, tossing back her cascade of black hair.

"It is my understanding that Blake Sullivan was living with you for several years?"

Juan looks at his wife, then back at me. "Nearly eight years."

"When was the last time you heard from him?"

They exchange another silent glance. It's apparent that they would rather eat a dozen lemons than talk about Blake.

"We haven't. No contact. Nothing," Juan insists, while Rosalita shakes her head vehemently.

I feel overwhelmed by being in the same place my brother spent eight years of his life. I can barely form a coherent sentence.

"Do you have a picture of him? I couldn't help but notice that there are no photos of Blake in your home."

Rosalita does the sign of the cross, and Juan twists at his mustache with his fingers. "What did the boy do this time?" Juan asks, ignoring my observation.

"He's been missing for nearly nine years."

Rosalita crosses her chest again and whimpers. Juan shoots her a stern look.

"My wife loved that boy very much. He was a good kid. My Breanna loved him too. He was good to her."

"What can you tell me about the assault he was doing time for in prison?"

"Dunno. He was with the wrong people. He . . . I don't know. I wasn't there."

Juan nervously fidgets with his fingers; my questioning must be opening up old wounds or have touched a nerve. His uneasiness rubs off on me, and my palms begin to sweat.

"How did Blake end up living with you?" I look down at my notes to calculate the year he moved in with the Sotos. After considering the time he spent in prison, a startling discovery shocks me. "He was still a minor, wasn't he?"

"Yes, sixteen," says Rosalita in her thick Spanish accent. "His aunt was a nightmare. She used drugs, *drink* too much, she . . . she *smoke*." Rosalita counts on her fingers for dramatic effect, and it works because I can picture the woman clearly. "She was no good. No kindness. No love. No care. No nothing."

Juan puts a hand on his wife's knee to calm her. I watch their interaction with envy. If I get teary-eyed during a sad movie, Doug tells me I'm being ridiculous for crying over a Hollywood film. When my favorite grandmother died, Doug got drunk with my crazy uncles during the wake; he didn't even consider that I might need a shoulder to cry on.

"Blake's aunt . . . Was she his guardian before you?"

"Si. Si. His parents *die* a year or two apart." She looks at her husband for confirmation.

"James Sullivan drowned while the family was vacationing at the beach. I believe it was in Encinitas or Carlsbad, I'm not sure," Juan elaborates. "Then his mother died a year later from brain, or some other type of, cancer."

I scribble the information down in my notepad, trying to hide my emotions. I'm here as a professional investigator, not a relative of the individual in question.

I look up from my notes, opening my eyes wide to hold back the tears. "What's the name of Blake's aunt? Do you know where I can find her?" I don't know Blake. I've never met him, yet I already feel connected to his life.

Juan sends his wife to the kitchen to find the aunt's contact information. Then, as if trying to avoid being alone with me in the room, he offers me a glass of water and leaves to get it before I initiate a conversation between the two of us.

I hear him pouring water from the tap. I can't drink it. My stomach is too sensitive. I only drink bottled beverages. I still smile and express my gratitude when he hands me the glass of water.

Rosalita appears with a note in her hand.

"This address is in Beaumont," I point out as I read the handwriting on the piece of paper. Barbara Sullivan: the same name listed as an emergency contact on Blake's penitentiary profile.

"Yeah," Juan points toward the east wall as if showing me the direction. "We used to live there. We moved to Hemet five years ago. I'm retired. I work part-time at a local indoor soccer arena."

"Makes sense. Thank you for the information." I copy the name and address onto my notepad.

"Can you tell me anything else about Blake? Who his friends were while living with you? How was his life? What kind of person he was?"

"No friends, only my Breanna. They were very close." Rosalita taps her hands together. "Like two eggs."

"He's been missing for nearly nine years. Do you have any idea where he might be? Any connections in Mexico perhaps."

Once again, the couple looks at each other in silence. Juan addresses me. "We didn't visit him in prison. He was having an affair with the woman he hit on the face. For years, Breanna was heartbroken. She didn't want to see him again."

The chiming of a cellphone interrupts our conversation. Rosalita gets up from the couch and leaves to answer it.

"The police were looking for him too. He might be dead, I don't know. There are no signs of him anywhere. He left prison, and that was the last time he was seen." I sense Juan is done talking to me.

"Can I speak with your daughter Breanna?"

He looks at his watch. "My daughter is at the soccer fields. Her kids have practice today."

He reaches for my notepad and writes the name of the park where she is at on it. "You must google the address. It's not far from here. On the other side of the train tracks. I'll tell her you are coming."

I nod and rise from the couch. "Thank you very much for seeing me, Mr. Soto."

He nods back.

As I walk out of the small charming home, I hear Rosalita talking so fast in Spanish that I have no chance to make out what she's saying.

13

The low-budget soccer arena is located behind an industrial park on a lot barely large enough for two enclosed fields with a strip of concrete for cars to park. If I had to come here after dark, I'd get the feeling that I could be kidnapped and sold for organs.

Overenthusiastic and loud parents hang on the edge of the wall that rings the turf soccer fields. If I didn't know better, I'd think these parents were cheering for a World Cup match.

I walk to a small shack with an open door, where I find a short, overjoyed Hispanic male with a round face and slick black hair. His smile never fades as he points me to the bleachers on the opposite side of the field, singling out Breanna Soto as the woman with bleached hair who is wearing a white dress.

I should have left my blazer in the car because I'm way overdressed for this crowd; I look too official. Soon my presence causes a mild panic. By the time I round the arena to the bleachers, a dozen or so cars empty the parking lot in a hurry.

The heavy air is stuck between the structures, and it's unbearably hot here. The chipped and uneven concrete emits a reeking, dry heat. My shoes aren't the best insulators, and I'm painfully aware of the heat radiating underneath my feet.

Short benches, four levels high, stretch out on the bleachers—a botched structure with aged and peeling blue paint. Faded banners hang on the back post tiredly advertising to the spectators in Spanish.

"Breanna?" I call out to the large woman wrapped in a tight cotton dress and clutching a baby.

She measures me up and down, then nods slightly.

"Did your father call you to tell you about me coming here?"

She nods again and wipes her nose with the back of her hand. Her makeup is astonishingly heavy and detailed. Her face is a marble statue with a colorful mask, one for a magazine cover. I try to picture her as a sixteen-year-old teen, lovestruck by my brother.

"Do you mind if I ask you a few questions about Blake?"

She shrugs, lays the baby over her shoulder, and motions me to a spot next to her.

I watch her small hand ending in long, bright fake nails holding the baby's back.

"How old is she?"

"Eight months," she says in an American accent. She chews her gum with gusto and yells at her kid on the field to run faster before she returns her attention to me. "I dunno whatcha wanna know about Blakey. I don't care about that fool no more."

I decide to get to the point. My company seems to irritate her as she keeps checking if others are watching us or not. "I'm trying to uncover any details about Blake

Sullivan's childhood. I'm trying to get a better picture of his possible whereabouts."

"He's likely dead. Buried in the desert somewhere," Breanna says plainly, void of emotion.

Her statement punches me in the chest. "What makes you say that?"

"It's been years. I'm no expert, but if someone has been missing that long, that usually means they're dead."

"Well, let's assume that he is alive for the time being. I understand that the two of you were very close."

She chuckles and shakes her head. "That was when I was young and stupid and still believed in love."

Judging by her posture and tone, I can tell her past is still haunting her.

"Can you tell me anything about his life when he was living with his aunt?" I look at my notes to look more professional, although I've already memorized the woman's name. "Barbara Sullivan."

Breanna snorts and switches the baby to her other shoulder. "She was a piece of work. She wasn't worthy of shoveling horseshit in a stall."

"How long was Blake under her guardianship?"

"I'm not sure." She bounces her knees up and down. "After Blake's mother died, on and off for ten years or so, until Blake finally emancipated himself."

"What do you mean by 'on and off'?"

She leans forward, screaming toward the arena. "Josh, start hustling!"

There is a group of thirteen elementary-school-aged kids running around the field, chasing a battered soccer ball.

A hard expression settles on Breanna's face. "Child services took Blake away a few times. Like four times. Maybe five. He was placed with other families."

Her jawbone repeatedly juts out against her face as she aggressively chews her gum. I'm sure it's me who is making her nervous.

"Do you remember the name of any of those families?"

She looks down at a few parents standing on the ground and leaning against the fence of the arena as if calculating the possibility of being overheard. "No, but some of them were bad, really bad," she says in a low voice.

I tap my notes with the tip of my pen "Can you be a little bit more specific."

She bobbles her head like a doll in the windshield. "Oh, it's the details you want. He was molested, okay? Raped. This one family solicited him for money. By the time his CASA caseworker found out about it, he had taken it in the *culo* dozens of times!"

My stomach flips. I don't know Blake Sullivan, but if the things I'm learning about him are true, I'll condemn my parents for abandoning him.

I pretend to search my notes. "I didn't find any record of that in my reports."

"Well, did you even look?" Breanna gives me an incredulous look. "Go down to Riverside County Social Services. They'll tell you. Flash them your shiny badge."

We are starting to attract more attention. I remove my blazer and drape it over my arm. I feel as if I'm suffocating in this heat. My mouth is dry. I should have drunk the water Juan Soto offered me. I clear my throat to help me talk.

"Did his aunt know about the sexual assaults committed against Blake?"

"Of course, she knew! That bitch didn't care . . . Only cared about where her next high would come from."

"There was no one else in the family to take care of Blake after his parents passed away?"

"I don't think so. Blake's parents were old. I mean they were like over fifty when they had him. They adored him, though. Spoiled him rotten. I always had a feeling Blake blamed his mother for dying so early and leaving him without protection. After Mr. Sullivan drowned in the ocean, Blake's mom started smoking, drinking, and popping pills. She completely lost touch with reality. Blake felt like she betrayed him . . . Then his aunt betrayed him over and over."

The baby starts getting fussy, and Breanna begins nursing her. Behind us, an adolescent boy has his face buried in the screen of a cell phone, smudging the screen with his fingers covered in Takis dust. By the sound of it, he is watching some goofy video.

"Was anything done about the crimes against Blake by the authorities?"

Breanna orders the boy behind us to turn the volume down on his phone, then stretches out her legs and repositions the nursing baby.

"Not much. Social Services got Blake away from the families that hurt him, but the damage was done. Were they prosecuted? That I don't know."

"Did any family take good care of Blake?"

"There was one family Blake loved a lot. I don't remember their names, but Blake often talked about them. They cared for him and treated him like one of their own. Although he only spent a few months with them, if I remember right. His aunt wanted him back."

I feel ashamed of our badly broken foster-care system, the kids yanked right and left in and out of homes like ragdolls. I can't imagine how frightening it must have been for young Blake to sleep in a strange bed in a strange house, fearing if someone would enter his bedroom to hurt him. Always having to live with uncertainties, not knowing when you will get a decent meal or who to trust.

For a moment, I contemplate how different my life would have turned out if my parents had given me up instead of Blake. The connection I'm developing with this troubled man is deepening. His life would have been mine if I'd been abandoned too. As if I had two lives. The life where I was loved and cherished and the life Blake lived, where he was abused and neglected.

There is much more I want to ask Breanna, but I don't think I can take any more of her stories and the heat for the moment. I thank her for her help and leave my card with her. I ask her to call me if she remembers anything else.

I walk back to my car, crank up the air conditioning inside, and drive away. I pull over a few miles down the road, near a dairy farm where cows chew the cud, and I throw up on the side of the road.

14

I'm in the restroom of a small gas station only a few miles away from the backroad ditch where I emptied my stomach contents. The modern tile design and stainless-steel appliances suggest this place has been recently refurbished, but penned and carved graffiti already deface the walls and doors. One toilet is clogged with paper, and the other is leaking water at the joint below, oozing over the dirty flooring. The air reeks of urine mixed with the fragrance of a cheap air-freshener set on top of the paper towel dispenser. It's not a pleasant place to be, but at least I'm alone.

I set my phone and keys on the only dry spot on the counter that has been spared from splashes of water, wet towel pieces, and spilled soap and wash my face. I rinse my mouth with a bottle of water I purchased at the convenience store while I was getting gas, then answer Anaya's call that's been blowing up my phone.

"Where are you?" she asks. It was only yesterday I saw her, but her clipped Britishness comes through, compared with the accents around here. "Do you have a moment to talk?"

"Hey, yes. I'm getting gas. What's up?" I try to sound casual as I wipe my face with a paper towel.

"Can you talk about what happened at the office yesterday?"

I take a hard look at my face in the cloudy mirror. "There was a misunderstanding during my background check that needs to be cleared up. What did you hear?"

The sound of a forced exhalation resonates through the receiver. "You know how this place is. If you don't tell the truth to people, their imaginations run wild."

"Do I want to know what the gossip about me is?"

"Probably not," she scoffs. "But I did overhear an agent who was reporting about a telephone interview with your parents that's been arranged for Friday. I think he was talking to the chief, but I'm not sure."

"Who was it?"

"Some dinosaur named Ted."

Great, just what I need. An old-fashioned hardhead who has no understanding or patience for anything outside his social norms.

"Well, I got nothing to hide. Agent Ted can investigate away," I say with conviction, yet my stomach is in a knot.

"As much as I want to know what's going on, I understand you can't talk about it." Anaya allows a moment to pass in silence, her final attempt at giving me a chance to share more information. When I don't respond, she concludes our conversation and sighs in disappointment. "Anyway, I hope things clear up for you soon so we can have you back in the office. The deadline is putting a real squeeze on us."

"I'll do my best, Anaya. Trust me, I wish I could be there with you. But hey, call me if you have any questions for me, okay?"

"All right. Let's keep in touch. And hey, don't hesitate to reach out to me if you need help. I'm here for you."

I hear incomprehensible chatter in the background and a door closing. I picture Anaya sitting in our special-operations office, and my heart skips a beat. An overwhelming sense of failure settles on me. I know I can't keep up the acting much longer. "Will do," I say. "Thanks for calling. I really appreciate your concern." I'm about to hang up when I realize I have the means to reciprocate her support. "By the way, do you have any plans for tomorrow? Doug and I are having a little get together. We can see the fireworks a few blocks from our house."

"Awww, thank you! I wish I could, but I've already made arrangements to go home and visit family."

"Well, enjoy yourself. I'll see you back in the office, I hope," I add with a short, frustrated chuckle.

I hang up the phone and gaze at my reflection in the restroom's mirror, going over the new developments in my head. My parents won't be able to lie during an FBI interview. My mother thought she had the right to deflect my questioning earlier, but I hope she's smart enough to come clean with the Bureau. I'm not sure what scares me more: my parents being interrogated by the FBI or finding out the truth.

It's approaching two o'clock in the afternoon, which means I ran out of time, so I opt to drive home instead of visiting Barbara Sullivan. Even if I leave right now and miraculously evade heavy traffic on the freeway, I still won't make it home by four as I promised Doug. The dread of an inevitable confrontation weighs me down as I walk back to my car. Before I roll out of the parking lot, I arrange a grocery delivery over the internet to save some time for cleaning the house. When I get back on the road, I feel overwhelmed, underappreciated, and most of all, downright out of luck.

15

As Doug's friends began to arrive at our house for the Fourth of July party, we both already have our welcoming and smiling faces on, putting the previous hour of bickering on the backburner.

It wasn't a spontaneous argument. Doug was upset with me from the beginning of the day.

I arrived home late last night to a chillingly vacant house, feeling mentally and physically exhausted. By the time I put away the lukewarm groceries I had found on the porch, ate dinner, and showered, I had no energy left to do much else. I spent the remaining hours of my evening sitting on my bed and going over Blake Sullivan's file again, hoping to find a clue I may have missed to his current whereabouts. But there was nothing in those files to point my investigation in a new direction. At that point, interviewing people from Blake's past seemed the only logical step to take.

I have a faint memory of Doug stealthily climbing into bed with me just before midnight, reeking of cigarette smoke and beer breath. I pretended to sleep to spare us both an unpleasant argument.

In the morning, we both overslept. I took the blame for not setting the alarm in silence so I could get on with tidying up of the house.

But the cleaning didn't go too well as I lacked focus and dedication to the task at hand. I was all over the place, jumping from doing laundry, preparing dishes, and cleaning bathrooms. Naturally, nothing was completed in an orderly fashion, and I felt I was making little progress. My house growing up was always clean and organized, a skill I never seemed to acquire. My mom should have passed down the secret art of tidying up to me before I flew from the nest. I guess she did try to teach me; I just wasn't paying attention.

On the other hand, Doug is a master at managing his time. He worked relentlessly, mostly out in the back, mowing the lawn and setting up the tables and chairs on the patio. Every time he came inside for a cold drink, he appraised my progress with the rolling of his eyes or a heavy sigh. An hour before the party started, he ripped the vacuum cleaner from my hand and sent me to make myself look presentable, reminding me that this party was my idea.

Doug's business partner, Ethan, was the only guest I was actually eager to see. He was one of the last to show up at the party; by then, I had become worried he might have found something better to do than to hang with us. At the sight of him, a rush of relief washed over me.

"Hey, Vic," Ethan leans in to hug me as I hold the door open for him. His lumberjack-inspired beard tickles my cheek. I relish the scent of his cologne as I return his embrace.

"I'm glad you could make it," I say, pulling away swiftly; Doug is approaching us.

"My man!" Doug whoops in with open arms for his best friend. He scoops Ethan away from me and leads him toward the patio, cutting through the crowd of people, who, despite eating my food and drinking my booze, never make an effort to get to know me.

I fix a smile on my face and check on the tray of pigs in a blanket baking in the oven. The uniform little mounds have turned golden brown. I unload them onto a dish and head to the backyard to place them on the table.

"Vicky!" Doug beckons me to a group of people encircling him like vultures. His fan club includes three women I have never met in person, but recognize from his Instagram posts, and some others I've met before, like Angela and Christine from the office, Ethan, and a tall, slim man with Asian features whose name I can't recall.

"I need your help, please save me," Doug swoons.

I step next to him, and he loops his arm around my shoulders.

"What seems to be the problem," I ask, smiling at my boyfriend as we are under scrutiny.

"My friends are asking me how we met, but you are a much better storyteller than I am, so please take center stage." Doug plays this intro with his usual theatrical flair. As the youngest of three brothers, born nearly a decade after the second son, he was the baby of the family. Doug's constant need to prove himself hasn't waned as an adult. His drive to do more and be more was what I adored in him, but learning how he's willing to lie to make himself look better tarnished my image of him. Yet I am his partner in crime because that's what couples do—they get each other's back.

There is nothing unique or #Instaworthy about how Doug and I met. Consequently, Doug doesn't like to talk about it. He made up a silly story about us crossing paths in a bar on Saint Patrick's Day and being tricked into love at first sight by a leprechaun. In reality, we stumbled across each other on an online dating site. Like most ordinary people, we, too, went out for dinner for our first date, then again, and again. After two weeks of eating and talking, Doug invited himself back to my apartment and stayed the night.

Every little detail between us seemed to click as if we were part of the same puzzle. Doug was my door to freedom and joy. He got me into running around the neighborhood in the mornings before work. And soon enough, Doug's love for outdoor activities, especially hiking and snorkeling, had rubbed off on me.

At the three-month mark of our relationship, Doug gave up the apartment he rented with two of his friends and moved in with me because it made sense financially. It worked out. Life was good together.

After being on the force for eight years, I was promoted to detective, and the increase in my pay allowed us to upgrade to our current charming little two-bedroom house located close to the beach. The excitement of starting a new chapter in our lives drove us on and kept our relationship strong.

But there is no light without darkness.

When the housing market crashed in southern California, Doug lost his job as a sales representative for a pool-construction company and couldn't find another job in that area of expertise. He decided to venture into new waters and obtained his realtor license. My paycheck had to stretch far enough to put Doug through school and finance his endeavors as a rookie agent. Money was tight: we could no longer afford to go on fun trips and enjoy the things in life we wanted to do. I worked as much overtime as I could to prevent our lifeboat from sinking, and Doug slowly increased his real-estate listings. We managed to survive those few tough years.

Doug is now a social-media star and a hotshot agent. We could afford to return to our former exciting lifestyle, but neither of us seems motivated to do so. Sometimes I wonder what went wrong between us.

Now here we are, keeping up appearances and telling lies to people to prove how happy we are.

The period of awkward silence drags on in the room. Doug must be sensing my hesitation and responds by coercing me to play along before his fan club grows suspicious. I give in and recite the made-up romantic story about how fate steered us together, keen to pay attention to the details. Some of these people already heard the story.

"Remember, Doug, you followed my girlfriend's car; she was taking me home from the bar, then you picked me up in secret and drove us to the beach?"

Doug kisses my cheek and tightens his grip on my shoulder—a reaction that receives a swoon of approval from his friends.

"The car's tire became stuck in the sand," Doug always adds that bit to make him look like a romantic soul. "We were too embarrassed to call for a tow truck, so we had to push the car out of the sand on our own, remember?"

I smile, and it's a genuine smile. We've told this lie so many times, I now believe it.

Doug did try to be romantic in the beginning, although I'm not sure he knew what he was doing. But that's not why I fell in love with him. His go-getter attitude and relentless energy toward life made me fall for him. He inspired me to better myself, and his enthusiasm was contagious. His love for life gave me an interruption from my responsibilities and taught me to relax. He helped me understand that the world had as much beauty in it as evil, if not more. I never forgot Susie and her killer, who was never caught, but I did learn to allow myself to enjoy a sunny day at the beach without feeling remorse. Doug taught me to compartmentalize my life, to oversee the balance of good and evil in my mind. I'll be forever grateful to him for that.

I steal a glance at Doug's face, stretched with pride as he wraps up our story. I think I still love this man, although I'm not sure. My feelings seem to be tangled lately.

"Did you guys know Vicky is an FBI agent?" Ethan blurts out without warming up the audience to a change of subject.

It's a statement that requires a few moments to marinate, but once it does, I'm bombarded with questions and expressions of amazement.

"I had no idea," says the brunette breathlessly. "How cool!" The young, attractive woman bursting with confidence punches Doug in the chest. "How come you never told us that your girlfriend is a special agent?"

Doug shifts on his legs, his pale face cringing. "I thought I did."

"Are the criminals getting smarter, Agent Collins?" Ethan continues, despite the obvious disappointment on Doug's face. "I read somewhere that the number of serial killers has declined in recent years. Which means that the perpetrators are either getting better at hiding their tracks or you guys are better at catching them faster."

"Well, all the crime shows and available information online about forensic science definitely has made our job harder. The media is educating criminals."

"She can't talk about her job, Ethan, you know that," Doug chimes in, stepping away from the circle in an attempt to break up the group.

I have no intention of stealing Doug's spotlight, so I second his warning.

I excuse myself by saying that it's time for desserts, and I head for the kitchen by myself. I remove the store-bought pies from the refrigerator and start popping off the tops when I sense someone behind me. I turn around. It's Ethan.

"Wanna join me for a smoke?" He flashes me a pack of Marlboro Lights poking from his pocket.

I'm not a smoker, but Ethan and I have this special tradition we've always shared. I enjoy his company because he loves hearing about my job. We could talk for hours about criminology because he's always shown a genuine interest in my work. In Doug's company, I feel the need to hold back, play it down, but with Ethan, I can be myself.

We go out front to the street and sit down on the curb. Ethan lights my cigarette, and I wash down the taste with my Bacardi and Coke. I developed a liking for this economical drink in college and I never cared to change to something more sophisticated.

"You're unusually quiet today," Ethan observes. "What's wrong?"

"Nothing special. I just have a lot on my mind."

"Working some big cases lately?"

"Yeah, you could say that." I smile at him. I usually avoid looking into his eyes because it's hard not to get lost in the azure blue, but I gaze into them now. "That thing that's growing on your face always looks so well-groomed. What's your secret?"

He crosses his legs and leans back, chuckling. "I have a rigorous grooming method. You wouldn't believe how many products are involved if I told you."

"I wish you would shave it all off once so I could see your face."

He runs his fingers down his beard. "It would feel like losing a limb."

"You are too handsome to cover a face like that." I don't know why I blurted that out, it was a mistake.

Ethan stares into my eyes. "Maybe I don't want to get noticed."

I take a long pull from my glass to deflect and watch him put out his cigarette on a smidgen of moist dirt between the curb and sidewalk. "I heard you're hunting a guy."

I sigh. "Doug and his big mouth, huh?"

"Don't be mad at him. It's guy talk. He means no harm."

I push the glowing ashes into the dirt too. "Have you ever heard the name Blake Sullivan?"

"Sullivan?" Ethan muses, gazing at the fading sky. "I can't say I have. Why?"

"Forget it. It's not important. This drink is messing with my head." I rub my forehead as I pour the rest of my drink down the gutter.

Ethan puts his hand on my thigh. "Is everything okay between you and Doug?"

My face flares up. "Yeah, we're good. Why?"

"Only asking for a friend," he laughs, and I can't help but laugh with him. Staying here with this charming man any longer could be dangerous. Ethan's gravitational pull is becoming too strong to resist. I sometimes imagine being with Ethan instead of Doug, but I could never stoop that low to date my boyfriend's best friend.

A car drives by, and the warm air of its wake envelops me. It enhances the dizziness in my head. I gaze at Ethan, and he leans in to kiss me. I don't push him away. I don't return the gesture either, I simply close my eyes and let his soft lips pepper mine.

He pulls away. "I'm sorry. I don't know what came over me."

I suck in my lower lip to taste him. "I think we'd better go back inside."

His red tongue runs over the surface of his lips. "I think you're right."

For the rest of the night, I make a point of staying away from Ethan. But during the fireworks, I lock eyes with him a few times, which prompts me to loop my arms around Doug's waist and kiss him. He doesn't like to be affectionate in public, so our kiss turns out to be awkward. For the first time in a long time, I have a gut feeling Doug is cheating on me. Suddenly, the kiss I shared with Ethan doesn't make me feel so guilty.

MEREDITH FALCONE'S LAST DANCE

My biceps flex and strain as I do my pull-ups on the bar hanging from my bedroom door, trying to work out my restlessness. "Twenty-five, twenty-six—" I count out loud over the soft humming of the fan. The air conditioning would cool down the temperature in my condo, but I need the suffocating warm air to sweat out my frustration.

"Thirty-two, thirty-three—" I count between clenched teeth, squeezing out the remaining power from my arms.

My bare feet give off a faint thud as I drop to the floor. I drink thirstily from a water bottle, feeling the tightness in my neck and upper back. It's a constant, uncomfortable feeling that's embedded deep into my tissues, driving me mad. At this late-night hour, there are no respectable places open to get a massage, so I must find another way to get rid of this numbing pain.

Meredith's face flashes across my mind for the umpteenth time, and I grunt with rage as I clamp my head between my hands. "Leave me alone! Leave me the fuck alone!" I yell, down on my knees. I don't want to see her. I don't want to talk to her.

I don't want to hurt her.

For the third time, I take a cold shower, hoping it will help clear my head. It does, but only for a little while.

Lying on my back in bed, I watch the blades of the fan rotate around, trying to hypnotize me.

I'm restless. I'm anxious. I'm hurt.

I reach for my laptop on the nightstand to look at Meredith's Instagram page. She's changed her profile bio since yesterday: *"Remember, at the end of the day the number one person you must love is you!"*

"Bitch!" I blurt out, scrolling down her recent photos with shaking fingers. Every single one is a selfie. Even if she posts a picture of her little girl, it's still a selfie of Meredith with her daughter in the background.

"Narcissist bitch!" I grunt as I slam down the screen of my laptop. I push it to the edge of the bed, knowing that there will be no sleep for me tonight.

I pull my research from the desk drawer and violently massage my aching right shoulder. I feel like someone is living inside of me—an alien crawling underneath my skin. No matter what I do, I can't get rid of this nagging feeling.

My index finger follows the lines as I run over my list. Everything seems to be in order—has been for weeks. I no longer have the self-restraint to postpone what I must do. "What you can do today, don't leave for tomorrow," my father used to tell me.

I'm doing it tonight.

Armed with purpose, I secure the paperwork and the burner phone in a portable safety box. After locking it with a pin code, I place it in my backpack. I throw on a faded t-shirt and a pair of athletic shorts. I step into my running shoes and head out.

I jog along the lit streets to my storage unit, located about two miles from my home. The low-security facility allows me to access my storage without checking in, which is why I chose this place. The lighting has always been mediocre in the east wing of the building, but since I broke the nearest lightbulb last year, which the management hasn't replaced yet, only a faint orange glow illuminates my path.

I push the gate up to access my belongings. Inside is a white sedan registered to Bill Champ, a fifty-four-year-old homeless man living in the dark alleys of Los Angeles. It's a three-year-old Honda Accord—one of the most popular cars in the area. It also can't be traced back to me.

After I get into the driver's side, I reach back and check under the seat for the duffle bag. My fingers touch the coarse fabric. Still there. I'm all set.

Instead of using an online navigation service that leaves a digital footprint, I use an ordinary old-fashioned map to find my way to Meredith.

On the road to San Marcos, I don't listen to music; I don't need any pacifier. The restlessness is gone. Now that I have a specific goal in mind, my focus is aimed and sharp.

I park five blocks from Meredith's home, next to a giant pepper tree for extra coverage. The street light closest to me is out. I took care of it a few days ago. In this part of the town, changing a lightbulb takes about a week. I know. I've tested this.

I remove my black leotard bodysuit from the duffle bag and change into it. The eye area is the only part of me that remains exposed after I pull on my gloves. I compared the shoe impression that was lifted from a series of home invasions in this neighborhood by the police to match the soles of shoes I purchased in a thrift store. I spent the extra time to create the same wear patterns shown in the forensics evidence file I acquired on the internet. It's not a perfect match but close enough.

The shoe is a size and a half smaller than my feet, and I wince as I pull them on, but I'll manage.

Once I make sure the streets around me are empty, I slip out of my car and creep along the shadows of the trees and houses to get to my destination.

On Wednesday nights, Meredith always leaves her daughter with her mother while she works the night stripping. She's brought home a different guy nearly every night I've had her under surveillance. I only hope tonight will be different. My plan won't work if someone else is in the picture.

To stop myself from worrying about things that may not happen and keep my focus, I check the time on my phone. It's 1:37 a.m. When I left home, I gave myself enough time for delays, which haven't occurred thus far, so I have plenty of time to fortify myself mentally. Once I embark on a hunt, I become the predator. Going home without killing my prey isn't an option. I failed once and almost went mad during the aftermath. I felt as if a loose end of a rope was dangling against my chest and face all day long. It took me months to shake the feeling.

Tonight, I'm a man on a mission once again. A real man. A tough man. I'll prove it to this little bitch that I'm not some soft puny toy for others to play with. I screwed it up with her this past spring when she tried to hit on me at a bar. She said it was cool to be gay. I'm not gay! I'm a man, like my father. One day, I'll get married and have kids who I will love and won't abuse. The only problem is that I can't find one decent woman in this country worthy of being a mother.

I have to give credit to Meredith for having the sense to take her daughter to a safe place before letting strangers into her home, but she is rotten all the same. Her little girl deserves better. Based on my research, Meredith's parents have more than enough money to support their daughter through community college so she could raise her little angel in peace. That means Meredith purposely chose this despicable lifestyle to spite them. She had the support to make something of herself, but she wants to be scum. Then I'll treat her like scum.

A pair of headlights beams through the dark street. I pray it's the old beat-up Mercedes C-Class with the broken taillight Meredith drives, because I'm starting to lose my head.

It's her, and she is alone. She is imbalanced on her feet as she staggers from the car to her front door, fumbling for her keys. She must be drunk or high, or both. She could have killed herself driving intoxicated, condemning her daughter to grow up an orphan. The woman wants to die. Don't worry, Meredith, I'll help you with that.

I silently follow her to the entrance, but she is too dazed to notice me. As the door cracks open, I push her inside the dark foyer. She falls forward, but I catch her before she hits the floor. There is a strict order of injuries she must suffer before she dies. I'm not the mastermind of this crime, only a humble follower.

Terror brings her eyes into focus. The seriousness of the situation immediately sobers her up. I wonder what she must be thinking as I hold the cloth over her mouth and nose. Is she praying to God for help? Is she making promises that she will change her lifestyle if she survives this attack? Maybe both? Maybe she is just wondering why her? Perhaps nothing at all.

As the effects of the chemicals take their toll, her eyes roll back, eyelids lower, and she goes limp in my arms. I gently lower her body onto the laminate floor and begin rolling her in stretch wrap from neck to ankles. Then, I pull out a knife and my checklist and go to work.

16

As I lie submerged in a few inches of water, I'm violently shaken like a ragdoll by someone whose face is dark and blurred to the point I can't make out any features. Stiff fingers dig into my flesh, lacking kindness or empathy. Over the splashing sounds, echoing voices bounce off the ripples of water in my flooded ears, struggling to hear the words. I think someone is telling me to wake up, but I lack the will to engage. I don't fight back. My mind refuses. It's so not like me to allow someone to treat me this way, but I do. An icy cold splash shocks me into awareness, and with a robust intake of air, my eyes snap open, and I violently sit up.

Doug is leaning over me. I stick my hands into the mattress to raise my head higher before I drown. As my brain processes the information, I realize that it was all a bad dream.

"Finally," Doug grunts, setting the empty glass on the nightstand.

I feel my chest. My shirt is drenched. "Did you just pour water on me?"

"I couldn't shake you out of your nightmare! How many Bacardis did you have last night?"

"Two. I didn't even finish the second one."

Doug throws a bathrobe onto the bed next to me. "There's an agent from the FBI here to see you."

I'm in no condition to talk to anyone, especially a coworker or my boss. My whole body feels as if a train ran me over last night. I'm dumbfounded because I have no recollection of going to bed after Doug and I returned home from watching the fireworks.

"Did you get a name?" I ask, pushing my feet into a pair of slippers. It's a task I struggle to accomplish because one of the slippers keep sliding away from me. Did I have a stroke last night that paralyzed one side of my body?

"I didn't catch her name. A slim black lady."

"Anaya," I breathe.

I pull my hair back and secure it with a clip. I tie the belt around my bathrobe and drag myself to the living room. I find Agent Reed sitting on the sofa, paging through a photo album she must have grabbed from underneath the coffee table.

The shuffling noise I make gives me away. Anaya looks up, and at the sight of me, her eyes shrink with surprise.

"Rough night?"

"You don't say," I whisper, trying to ignore my skull-splitting migraine. "I guess I'm living proof special agents are humans too. We go through the same miserable shit everybody else does."

Anaya raises the photo album in her hand. "You guys have been to some amazing places," she comments as she lays the booklet on the table.

"Used to. We're like an old married couple now," I groan. "Minus the marriage license, of course."

I don't know why I'm sharing personal matters with my work partner. I'm usually not the open-book kind of coworker.

Doug emerges from the kitchen and pushes a glass of fizzing water into my hand. "It's Airborne. It might help. I don't know."

I'm dizzy and need to sit down. I choose the farthest single seat from my friend. If I stink as bad as I look, I don't want to subject her to that discomfort. I never leave the house without showering. My mother nailed that into my head when I was a little girl. "You never know what happens once you leave the house. You might get into an accident and be transported to a hospital. You'd die of shame if you didn't have clean underwear on."

Anaya shifts uncomfortably. "I'm sorry for barging in on you like this. I must have called a dozen times, but you didn't answer."

"I might have muted my phone last night. Honestly, I don't remember," I say massaging my forehead.

She drops a file onto the table. "I think our Piggyback Killer has struck again. We have another body."

I've been so wrapped up in finding my alleged brother that the Piggyback Serial Killer we've been chasing slipped my mind.

"How do you know it's him?"

"We don't, but I have a strong feeling."

From the corner of my eye, I spot Doug eavesdropping.

"Where is the crime scene?"

"San Marcos."

"We've never had a victim this close to us before."

"True, and there's another inconsistency. A series of burglaries in the area for the past seventeen months. The perpetrator chose homes of women who lived alone and always hit the homes when nobody was there. About three weeks ago, a young woman was killed during what seemed to be a robbery."

She turns the report toward me and pushes the whole package to my hands. I see brutal crime-scene photos of a young woman lying in a pool of blood. The sight of blood never made me faint, but I'm balancing on the edge right now. Keeping the contents of my stomach down is a task I may not be able to tackle.

"The police connected the crime with all the other burglaries using footprints left behind the scene," she continues, though I'm sure she noticed how my face drained of color. "During the investigation, it became evident that the homeowner wasn't supposed to be home so early that night. A change in her work schedule equated to her return to her home at an earlier time. She likely surprised the intruder and paid for it with her life. Now the last victim—" Anaya glances at her notes. "Meredith Falcone returned home after 2 a.m. as usual. If the perpetrator did stalk her prior to the attack, as the police suspect he did with all the other victims, he must have known he had plenty of time to ransack the empty house before the victim returned home. It seems as if he was waiting for her so he could kill her."

"Predators evolve. Maybe he enjoyed the rush of killing three weeks ago and wanted the same adrenaline high again."

"Perhaps, but I think we should still drive out there and investigate."

"I'm on paid leave, remember?"

"Not anymore. The chief will call you, if he hasn't done so already."

"What changed his mind? He was rather adamant about me staying out of sight."

"When we got a call from the local PD about this case, Brestler convinced the chief that our special investigation is more important than a piece of missing information from your background check. The chief is reasonable. He agreed."

"How come I wasn't notified?"

"I'm sure he called you. Did you check your phone?"

I sip at the fizzy drink. "No, I didn't."

"How much time do you need to get ready?"

Never in my life have I felt so reluctant to go to work. It would take a miracle to look presentable on such short notice in my condition, but need drives me to act. "Thirty minutes? Maybe less."

"All right. I'll make you some breakfast," Anaya gets to her feet with a deep sigh. "Go jump in the shower. Brestler is meeting us there."

I slowly crawl out of my armchair. "I picked the right night to let loose, didn't I?"

I'm rewarded with her sweet smile. "As you said, we are human, like everybody else. Just don't mention it to Brestler. He's a bit more old-fashioned than I am."

I move my hand in a circular motion in front of my face. "Like Brestler won't notice this."

* * * * *

When I return, somewhat refreshed, Doug and Anaya are laughing loudly in the kitchen. It's a bit annoying to see them being so friendly as if this wasn't their first time meeting. Doug has a unique talent to strike up friendships with women in record time. I'm not armed with that skill set for the opposite sex.

I smell eggs and coffee. My stomach turns.

As excruciating as it is, I eat because I don't want to seem rude. As I poke at my egg, I can't get the sight of blood in the shower out of my head, wondering what kind of sex games Doug and I played last night, resulting in internal injuries to this extent.

A nagging feeling prompts me to pull Doug aside and ask him about last night, but Anaya keeps checking the time and urging us to get moving, so I don't have the chance to talk to Doug in private. If I want to get back into the good graces of the chief, I better hurry up and bring my best self to work today. We need to nail that son of a bitch before he kills again.

Doug puts his hand on mine as I place a dirty dish in the sink. "Don't worry about it, honey. I'll take care of it."

I give him an appreciative nod because Anaya is studying us, yet I can't help but watch him with suspicion. I don't remember ever waking up in such a pitiful state after a party, and I partied hard in college.

"Don't forget, I'm going to Irvine today. I won't be back until Sunday night." Doug's statement catches me at the front patio.

"Good luck!" I offer, pushing the strap of the laptop case up higher on my shoulder. "Don't forget to feed the fish before you leave."

17

naya gazes at me over her straight arm resting on the steering wheel as we crawl forward at a snail's pace north on Interstate 15. We are meeting Brestler and the local lead investigator assigned to the serial homicide cases that have been terrorizing San Marcos.

"You and Doug are so sweet together," Anaya says, smiling teasingly.

I find it interesting how people can make such a statement based on a snippet of information they observe in someone's life. I'm not complaining; I do the same. It's human nature, I guess. Maybe that's why most of us gravitate toward thrillers. We want to know what's happing behind closed doors. Our curiosity is a monster with an insatiable appetite that can never be satisfied. So, we pry and pry.

"We have our moments," I remark, not looking up from the paperwork spread across my legs. I'd rather not talk about my love life with Doug this morning. I may not say the things Anaya would want to hear. "How's Alex?" I ask, setting up a detour for our conversation.

Anaya's been dating a dental technician she was introduced to by a colleague of ours a couple of months ago. After their first date, the two of us stalked the guy online, hoping to uncover some dirty secret he's been harboring. There is no way a handsome forty-year-old man with a thick head of light brown hair and athletic body hasn't been able to find a match for himself all these years. He had to have a weird fetish or be a sexual deviant to keep the ladies from marrying him. To our surprise— maybe disappointment—we couldn't find anything incriminating on him. He was well-liked by his coworkers, an active part of the community, and coached youth flag football. He built houses for those in need with Habitat for Humanity and was the perfect man that every woman dreams of marrying. I couldn't have been happier for Anaya. Truth be told, I was a tad bit envious of her. That first wave of excitement and anticipation that washes over a new relationship is the best part of every relationship. Doug and I had already settled into a life of routine and habits, and we aren't even married. But since Anaya started dating this new guy, I lived through her stories, soaked up her enthusiasm, and fed on her energy.

My friend's hands slide down to the lower part of the steering wheel, and she arches her back. It's a posture indicating the beginning of an unhappy story.

"We don't see each other anymore," she says, chewing her gum violently. "We both have crazy schedules, and we just couldn't make it work."

"I'm sorry. You should have called me. We could have gone out for a drink and talked shit about him." I fix a feigned grin on my face.

My offer draws a faint smile onto my partner's lips. She glances at me, bobbing her head. "You're right. I should have told you. But there's no need to talk ill of him. He was a good guy. My cute little northern saw-whet owl. Our breakup was amicable. Very adult-ish."

"That's better, I guess, but it still sucks. Nevertheless, my offer for a drink still stands. Okay?"

"I may take you up on that."

We hit stop-and-go traffic again near Escondido and continue on Highway 78. While the seat in Anaya's Chevrolet Equinox is comfortable, sitting for this long is causing me discomfort. As my partner complains about lousy drivers holding up the traffic in front of us, I pull out my cellphone and text Doug, asking him about last night.

His reply: We didn't do anything we haven't done before.

Maybe I imagine things. The blood I washed away in the shower this morning might have been a random discharge between two periods. I tend to skip my annual doctor's visits, but I still look up information online regarding my health. Women my age complain about irregular menstruation cycles all the time, especially those who've never given birth. Shit, I feel old.

After a short stretch of silence, indicating that a change of topic is in order, Anaya turns to me and asks. "So, what're your thoughts on this homicide?"

"It's a tricky one. At first glance, it seems to me that a local perpetrator evolved from burglary to murder. It's not common, but it does happen. Meredith's murder is identical to the previous victim's murder. What was her name?" I flip through the pages. "Oh, here, Linda Osborne. But there's inconsistency in the way he selects his victims.

All the former victims were between eighteen and twenty-five, lived alone, no kids, single. However, Meredith was thirty-two and a mother. That raises flags for me. It initially appears to me that the perpetrator meant to commit the crime with minimal collateral damage to his victims. The evidence indicates he stalked each victim to find the perfect time to break into their homes when nobody was there. He had plenty of time to ransack the place. Linda Osborne was simply at the wrong place at the wrong time."

"Exactly. Linda's death doesn't have the premeditation angle to it. It was a crime of necessity, and the perpetrator had to improvise. Yet the second murder is identical to the first one. If this bloody cassowary did enjoy the first killing and decided to do it again, wouldn't he plan it the second time around? If he did, the two murders wouldn't have been committed in the exact same fashion, don't you think?"

She was right, of course. I could see her point. I may have come to the same conclusion myself if not for this spitting headache that kept tormenting me.

"What's a cassowary?" Knowing Anaya it must be another bird I've never heard of.

She motions with her hand. "It's a flightless bird living in Australia. Very aggressive. It's known to kill humans."

I smooth my hair back and take a deep breath. "All right. Let's assume this crime is the work of our Piggyback Killer. Now we need evidence to support the theory."

My phone buzzes. I show the screen display to Anaya.

She scoffs. "Right on time. We're almost there."

"Chief," I answer.

"Agent Collins, you are harder to reach than the president. Have you been spending your paid vacation fishing?"

Shit, he knows what I've been doing? "No, sir. I-I don't like fishing." Christ, Vicky! "I mean, I accidentally muted my phone and um, missed a few important calls this morning."

"Relax, Vicky, I'm messing with you. Anyway, I believe you already talked to Agent Reed this morning, so I'm calling to confirm that your return to the Bureau is temporarily approved. All the paperwork is on my desk." I hear a pounding sound as he must have brought down his fist onto a stack of paper. "Your team is assigned to investigate the murders in San Marcos. Please approach the locals with caution. It's primarily their investigation, not ours. You are there to collaborate, collect information, and bring everything back to the office for analysis. Understood?"

"Crystal clear, sir. Thank you."

"All right. I look forward to seeing what you three manage to gather. I hope Reed's suspicion pays off because I'm being pressured by D.C. We need more than theories about this so-called Piggyback Killer. We need proof. Understand?"

"Yes, sir. We won't let you down. That's a promise."

"That's what I like to hear."

Anaya is pulling a silent theater next to me, indicating I went overboard with kissing the chief's ass. I wave my hand at her to stop before I burst into laughter.

After I hang up, I gulp down two aspirins with half a bottle of water. I'm parched and feel weak. If I had such a good time last night that this is the aftermath, I wish at least I could remember it.

"See, you're more valuable to the Bureau than you may think," Anaya concludes, as we turn west on San Marcos Boulevard, placing us two minutes from our destination.

I have no response to her comment. I feel anything but valuable right now.

San Marcos is a city in the North County region of San Diego County, with plenty of restaurants, coffee shops, and parks. It's also a college town, housing tens of thousands of students—many for the first time in their lives without parental guidance. For experienced and cunning predators, these young adults, filled with a sense of invincibility but lacking caution, can be easy targets. I remember when I was in college, thinking the world was my oyster, that there was nothing I couldn't do. And while those feelings of empowerment helped me through my exams and early job interviews, they led me to do stupid things, like walking home alone from parties, rip-roaring drunk. The fact that I'd never fallen victim to sexual assault, never been kidnapped or murdered is a mere miracle. I came to appreciate my luck after working with homicide detectives during my time on the force. Not all girls were as lucky as me, like this young woman whose homicide we're investigating.

Based on the research I'm conducting on my laptop while Anaya is driving, murder is nearly non-existent in San Marcos; however, the frequency of sexual assaults and home invasions has increased in recent years. This case may be completely unrelated to our special investigation, merely a chain of events similar to the other homicides.

The possibility of linking the Piggyback Killer we've been chasing to Meredith's murder puts me on edge, especially when I'm hungover. I've become accustomed to hunting down offenders online during my time with the cybercrime unit for the police department, but the fieldwork aspect of the job is relatively new to me. I fear looking incompetent in front of experienced detectives, but luckily Anaya has enough confidence for the both of us, and for now, I'm okay working in her shadow.

Our crime scene lies in the Sunset Apartments, just off the boulevard. It's a bare, two-story rectangular building housing four two-bedroom condos. Meredith's door is concealed by a wooden staircase leading to the second floor and a row of hedges by the sidewalk—a likely reason the killer may have picked her.

Anaya pulls in next to a police cruiser, and we are immediately bathed in flashing blue lights. Yellow police tape stretches across the entire parking lot. A Hispanic woman is pulling on it as a uniformed officer is trying to keep her back. A small kid is crying on her hip, and two more young children are clinging to her thighs. I interpret the signs as a tenant trying to access her home.

"Here we go!" says Anaya as she opens her door. "Put on your game face. It won't be easy to get these old dogs to accept our authority."

"Happen to you before? It's my first field assignment. I wouldn't know."

"Yeah, look at us. I'm a black woman with a British accent and you are, well, you are a blonde. I can only imagine the stereotypes running through their heads right now!"

"I'm not blond, my hair is light brown," I correct her. "Let's ignore the politics and get the job done. I'm not going to get caught up in some bullshit pissing contest."

We make our badges visible as we approach the circle of men standing on the sidewalk near the staircase.

"Gentlemen, how are you?" Anaya's greeting is met with six sets of suspicious eyes.

"The press release will be this afternoon. No comment until then," says a round-faced pale man with a thick mustache.

"We won't miss it, thank you," Anaya says professionally, then holds up her identification. "I'm Special Agent Anaya Reed and this is Special Agent Vicky Collins from the FBI's San Diego office. I believe you've been notified about our arrival?"

A sudden change in the air is palpable. Some of the men in the circle make excuses to leave, others step closer to us.

A bald man with thick muscular arms offers his hand. "Sorry about the confusion. I'm the lead investigator on this case. Detective David Brown from the San Diego County Sheriff's Department. One of your agents is already here. We didn't expect more of you."

The wailing of the Hispanic woman suddenly fills the air. She's broken through the police tape, and two officers are having to aggressively keep her back.

"Relative of the victim?" I ask.

"No. A tenant from Apartment 2A," Brown points to the second floor. "The building hasn't been cleared yet, so she can't return home."

"Did you find any evidence of the perpetrator making his way to the second floor?"

"No, nothing like that."

"Then what do you need to grant her access to her home? Those kids look hungry and tired. She may have no other place to go."

"Well, Agent Collins, is it? First, we need to collect all the footprints and tire marks around the building, then search every square inch of the outside for trace evidence—that includes the staircase as well. Once the CSI guys give me the green light, I'll grant the tenant access to her apartment," Brown says mockingly.

"Where are we in the investigation now?" Anaya cuts in, saving me from further embarrassment.

"We got a blood splatter specialist on the scene. He's inside right now with your agent. The rest? You need to talk to that man over there." Brown points to a white coverall-clad tall male, searching a forensic kit in the trunk of a black SUV.

"I'll meet you inside," I tell Anaya. I pull out my wallet as I approach the mom and children. I took Spanish in college, and although a bit rusty, I manage to convey she should spend some time at the Denny's across the street. I hand her forty dollars. She takes the money without saying thanks and ushers the kids toward the diner.

I return to the crime scene, and as I step in, Detective Brown calls after me. "I hope you haven't had breakfast yet. It's not a pleasant sight in there."

"Thanks for the warning," I smile at him to smooth over our initial hostile introduction. He responds with a meek "Good luck" and hands me a sick bag.

18

Brestler notices me in the foyer and waves me inside. The female crime-scene investigator logging evidence outside the door nods to confirm that the scene had been processed and I'm permitted to enter.

The first thing that hits me is the putrid smell of blood, urine, and some other unpleasant odor I can't identify. In the seconds following death, unintentional discharge of body fluids is common. However, the rancid odors don't deter me from moving toward the crime scene. As the oldest sibling growing up, I was in charge of cleaning the dirty bathrooms.

I take my time to catalog the state of the home on my way to the kitchen, where Brestler and Reed are conversing with two officials in white coveralls. The place has clearly been ransacked, although piles of clothes on the dirty floor and other masses of clutter are evidence that it wasn't a well-organized home to begin with.

A string of alpha-numeric yellow identification markers placed alongside bloody footprints leads me on my path. The body had already been taken by the forensic medical examiner in the early morning hours. In its place, hundreds of sticky-notes label the different types of blood spatters on the walls and furniture. Detective Brown was right: it is a freaking bloodbath in here.

"See all the castoff blood spatters?" Brestler speaks directly to me. "They all came from the assailant's knife as he repeatedly stabbed the victim." He imitates a series of stabbing motions with his hand, and from his performance, a chill runs down my spine.

"We won't know until the autopsy is complete, but judging by the number of different castoff spatters, I can confidently state the victim was stabbed at least a dozen times. Henry Shin. Blood Spatter Expert, San Diego County Sheriff's Department." A graying Asian man with a double chin, clad head-to-toe in white, introduces himself. He puts up his gloved hands, indicating we must skip shaking hands. It's not like I was going for it.

I squat down to examine the pool of dried blood on the tile floor. "Did the technicians find any usable fingerprints?"

Shin pulls the zipper down to his stomach. "The unit collected over a hundred fingerprints from the apartment. It will take time to eliminate the victim's fingerprints and anyone who had a legitimate reason to be in the apartment. I don't have high hopes of finding any foreign prints. The perpetrator has never left a print at prior scenes. He's likely wearing gloves to avoid leaving any."

"But you never know, right?" Reed instigates.

Shin raises his eyes to her and pushes his round glasses back into place. "Right. You never know."

"Do we have the time of death?" I ask.

Brestler flips a page on his notes. "Based on rigor mortis, the ME places the timeline between 1 a.m. and 5 a.m. on Thursday morning."

"We will have a more accurate time after the autopsy," Anaya informs me.

"Hell of a way to celebrate our Independence." My mind slips away to yesterday's party, where I was drinking, talking, and enjoying my time with friends, while this poor girl was fighting for her life. As our world gets more crowded, I swear not a second goes by without someone suffering. My job is hard enough without letting myself get distracted about dark places. Though I still feel dizzy and sick, I bring my mind back to the present.

I look up at my partner. "What do you think?"

Anaya is already focused like a hunting dog that's found a fresh scent on the trail. "The two crimes are too identical. This case can't be written off as the MO of a serial killer. It's an exact copy of the Osborne murder. Fits our copycat's profile." Anaya is getting herself worked up. She is committed. Passionate. That's why she is a damn good investigator.

"So you truly believe that the two crimes were committed by two different perps?" I ask.

Anaya smacks her lips. "I bloody believe so," she says and sips at her tea. "Linda Osborne must have been collateral damage. She came home at the wrong time. Her death was a mistake. The bloke just wanted to rob her place and not murder her. So why do it again?"

"He might have enjoyed the first kill and wanted to feel the rush again," I say with conviction. Anaya's theory was starting to make sense, but I still felt the need to argue. "So, he planned the attack on Meredith."

Anaya offers me her cup of beverage, but by the color of it, I can tell she put milk in her tea again. Too British for me, so I politely decline.

My partner's face fixes into seriousness. "If you killed someone by accident, a crime of desperation, yet somehow you enjoyed it and decided to do it again, wouldn't you do a cleaner job the second time around? Wouldn't you plan it better? I mean, look at this bloody mess?" Anaya points her pen at me. "Our Piggyback Killer has done this. I feel it in my guts."

I nod at my partner, "We still need proof."

I straighten back up and address the crime-scene investigator standing across from me. "The bloody footprint in the foyer, does it match the footprints collected at the previous crime scenes?"

He is a strong-built man in his late forties. His facial features remind me of Batman's archenemy, the Joker. His bushy eyebrows curve mischievously as he talks and the corner of his mouth rises high, creating a heart-shaped mouth lined with rows of big white teeth. He looks as if he is smiling, but he isn't. His thick mustache runs parallel with his hairline, making his face look somewhat rectangular. His dark locks of hair are secured into a tight manbun. He strikes me as a man devoted to his hobbies and interests, likely preventing him from ever starting a family.

"I only have the preliminary examination results at the moment, the findings have to be verified before I can say for sure."

"Off the record, if you have to take a wild guess?"

In a murder investigation, every element is equally important, like pieces of a puzzle. Even though some crime-scene investigators like to believe that their area of expertise is more important than others'.

The big man grimaces as he gives in to the pressure of our staring eyes. "The footprints we collected inside the apartment and around the perimeter of the property are consistent with the prints collected at the previous break-ins. A man's size nine and a half athletic shoe. Unfortunately, it's a common brand and widely available," he says in a monotone voice, not blinking.

"Did you ever release the image of the footprint to the media?" Brestler asks this essential question that makes me gaze at him with adoration. I've come to hold Brestler in high regard. The confidence and professionalism radiating from him give him an air of authority. His age is difficult to estimate because clean living and exercise keep him energetic, agile, and in great shape, while the worn skin on his face gives away that he's seen harsher days. Long scars and small blemishes give him a rough appearance that I found unattractive at first but that I've rather grown to like now.

"To the media? Of course not," says the CSI, offended.

Brestler massages the spot on his nose between his eyes. "Let's get back to the car. We need to talk."

"I'd like to stay for a while and take some notes. I want to get a feel for the victim's personality if you don't mind." I sound as if I'm asking permission to do my job. I should have constructed my sentence into a statement, not a request. I'm an FBI Special Agent. I'm here to investigate a serial murder case by any method necessary. No handholding needed.

Anaya opens the cover on her iPad. "I'm staying too. I need to take some pictures."

Brestler zips down his coveralls and tucks a pen inside his jacket pocket. "I'm going to grab a coffee across the street. I'll meet you two in the parking lot. Take your time."

I turn my focus to the job at hand. I meticulously observe the contents of the refrigerator. On food-stained and scratched-up plexiglass shelves sits an array of uncovered leftover microwave dinners, Styrofoam takeout boxes, a few beers, a jug of lemonade, and a single Yoplait low-fat yogurt. No fruits or vegetables. No milk or juice for her kid. The cupboards contain a vague collection of canned soups, boxed macaroni and cheese, and an open bag of Goldfish. A guaranteed recipe for developing cancer over time. Unwashed plates and cups are piled up in the sink and flies circle in the air above. There is no dish soap on the countertop, and I can't locate a dishwasher either.

A small round table and three chairs are nestled in the corner, laden with unopened mail and magazines. Blood drops are splattered on top of them, marked with forensics' sticky-notes.

I stop for a moment to put myself in Meredith's shoes. I try to determine what upbringing led her to this chaotic life. She may have been the youngest or the second to youngest in a line of siblings, likely growing up with few or no house rules and with a lack of parental supervision or guidance, leading to an early rebellious life, dating boys at a young age, and getting pregnant in her teens. Her dad may have been absent or broken down by life to care too much about yet another little girl. Many young girls who grow up with an alcoholic father who had a strained relationship with his children seek approval from other men.

I let my eyes linger on a photo of Meredith and her daughter on the mantel. It's a double selfie taken at the park at what seems to be a birthday party for another kid. She was a beautiful woman: olive skin, dark curly hair, sparkling green eyes. She probably didn't have a lot of close friends. Based on her career and the amount of clothing, shoes, and cosmetics I find in the apartment, I consider Meredith as someone who cared about how she looked; appearance seemed to be important to her. If friends did frequently visit her at home, I doubt she would have kept the place in such disarray.

The TV is missing from the stand, and the charging cables on the desk suggest her laptop was stolen, but there must have been little here worth taking. Why risk prison for a few bucks? Unless Meredith kept rolls of cash hidden somewhere, which would suggest her assailant knew her.

I jot down a note to myself about looking into her clientele at the gentleman's club, anyone who might have harassed her or been obsessed with her.

I catch Anaya entering the bedroom from the corner of my eye. "I'm done taking pictures. You need more time?"

"Something is bothering me about this victim," I say. "Look around! Why would anyone ever consider a home invasion in this low-rent, rundown apartment? There are no riches here worth stealing."

"I thought the same. That's why I asked you to come here and take a look. Meredith doesn't fit the previous victims' profile the guy's been targeting."

"Criminals can change their MOs. But to me, it seems, that here, Meredith was the primary target, and our guy opened a few drawers and took the TV to make it look like a robbery."

"Let's find Brestler, then we can head down to the PD. The homicide investigators from San Diego County will meet us there too."

"All right," I agree, closing up my notebook.

On my way out, my phone starts vibrating in my pocket. It's my mom. I hesitantly answer it.

"Victoria Emma Collins! I can't believe you set your FBI friends on me!" Mom's yelling hysterically on the other end. "Your fixation with finding something bad in your life has put our entire family in jeopardy!"

"What are you talking about, Mom? Why are you being so dramatic? I told you the FBI is investigating my background."

"Why can't you just be happy, Victoria? Please, tell me!"

"I *am* happy. This has nothing to do with me. I thought you knew about the phone interview with the Bureau."

"Apparently, your father set it up, and he isn't even here."

"Where is he?"

"Up in Utah, as I told you. He won't be back 'till tonight."

"I don't know what to say, Mom. This whole thing is out of my control. If you had told me the truth when I asked you, this whole situation could have been avoided, but you chose to keep secrets from me."

"What secrets? Why can't you let this go?"

"I have a brother I never knew. I don't know who he is or where he lives. But I know he's a criminal and had a hell of a tough time growing up. How could you throw him away, Mother?"

"I didn't throw anybody away! You need to stop saying that!"

"Then how can you explain what's going on?"

A long silence prompts me to call out to my mother three times before I hear her voice again.

"Well, I told everything I know to the FBI. The cat is out of the bag. Come and visit me when you can. I'll tell you what you want to know, although, I'm sure you'll find out the truth at work soon enough anyway. But Victoria, I must warn you. It will not be easy to hear the truth, let alone digest it."

My legs begin shaking, and I hold up two fingers to Anaya, indicating that I'll join her and Brestler in two minutes. Then I turn away, facing the apartment building. "I want to hear the truth now."

"No, not on the phone. We need to talk about this in person. Your father and I will be here all weekend. Come by anytime."

"You can count on it," I promise and disconnect the line without saying goodbye. I don't think I've ever hung up the phone on my mother. But I'm beyond angry now. I'm facing problems with Doug at home, my life is in shambles, and in the meantime, I'm chasing a copycat serial killer. The last thing I need is a gigantic family complication to add to the problems in my life.

I'm also disappointed in my father. After leaving three messages on his voicemail since my meeting with the chief, he hasn't called me back. I understand he's away for work, but there is no way he couldn't spare a moment of his time to talk to me. This is so unlike him. I'm always worthy of his time.

I stare at the screen of my iPhone for a moment. Then I do something I've never had to do before. I use the *find my phone* option on my cell to locate my father.

What I see leaves me breathless.

19

It's becoming impossible to do my job with my family sidetracking me with their dirty secrets and lies. I've been put on paid leave after being on the job for only three months because a long-lost brother of mine I've never met—never heard of—discredits me at work. Now my conscience is forcing me to leave a crime scene and my colleagues for a family emergency. I'll end up driving to a nearby city to investigate why my father's phone is in California instead of Utah, where he is supposed to be. If I keep this up, I'll go from the "new rising star" to a failed agent who never reached her potential.

I don't mean to complain or pass the blame. I was the one who made the decision to check on my father; no one forced me. I could have ignored the fact that he wasn't in Utah like he told my mother, and let my parents work out the problems in their marriage on their own, but digging for the truth is what I do, and that need drove me to follow my instincts.

Halfway to my destination, I comfort myself knowing that nobody has heard from my father for two days, and he may be in trouble, so I'm obliged to investigate. I use this excuse for abandoning my job as I pass along El Camino Real road, chasing my father's phone GPS on my Find my Phone app.

Although I live forty miles from Oceanside and I've driven by this small beach city numerous times on Interstate 5, I've never actually had the pleasure of visiting the place. Ethan has a neighbor whose kid comes up here to play in prestigious soccer tournaments. A few years ago, the city transformed a former landfill into an impressive sports complex. At one of the realtor mixers I attended with Doug, I overheard Ethan criticizing his friend for allowing her young son to perform intense physical activity during the hottest part of the day while inhaling toxic vapors that still fumed from the trash buried deep under the soccer fields. I didn't pay much attention to the woman's response, because I know nothing about children or youth sports, but I do remember how intensely Ethan argued with the mother. During their conversation, he became a vivid advocate for children, though he hasn't any of his own. He has never taken on the responsibility of being married either. But that's Ethan—the crusader for lost causes.

My Uber driver turns onto Mesa drive, where a robust chemical odor floods the car. I pin my nose looking up at the small plateau along the road blocking my view. The man behind the wheel must have seen me in the rearview mirror because he answers my question before I ask it.

"The new SoCal soccer complex is on the other side of the street, and next to it is a compost treatment facility. Sorry about the foul smell." My driver resembles a tech-savvy IT guru in Silicon Valley with a light gray V-neck cotton sweater, sleeves pulled up. The hair is completely gone from his egg-shaped head while dark stubble rises high on his cheeks and low on his neck, creating a collar for his long pointy nose that holds his black-rimmed glasses. He seems to be on edge, yet annoyingly friendly. He irritates me because it's a charade; nothing about him seems to be genuine. I do understand his need to pretend. It can't be easy to work for instant ratings that can make or break you.

"No worries," I assure him. I look down and start ripping a broken piece of nail from my thumb, indicating that I'm not up for talking.

We roll into a 55+ community where every street is named after a spice. At first sight, I find the area quaint and neat—prepackaged wealth and happiness for the last hurrah.

We climb a small hill and turn left onto Sesame Way. The dot I've been following for two hours has been marking a house only a few yards up ahead on the street.

I reach over the driver's shoulder. "Would you mind pulling over here?"

He follows my instruction without question.

"I'll be only a few minutes, then we can head back to San Marcos."

"That's fine. It's your money. I'll be here." He rewards me with a half-smile and releases the door lock.

I approach the house on the left with my iPhone in my hand. According to the app, my father is inside the single-story unit home.

The street is a canal of bare concrete with no trees or shrubs for cover. If my father steps out of the house, I'm a sitting duck.

A warm sweat is beginning to bead on my forehead from the combination of the sweltering heat and my nerves. I wipe it away as I casually walk by the target house and peek into the front yard. Behind a black wrought-iron gate, I see a paved sitting area decorated with an abundance of potted green plants and flowers. I hear water gurgling, but I'm too nervous to stop and look for the birdbath or fountain.

I hear laughter. The metal screen door is closed, but the entrance door behind it must be open. When I squint my eyes, I make out the shapes of people. There's a backdoor that's open on the other end of the hallway. The flooding sunlight turns the occupants into silhouettes.

I glance back at my Uber. The white Prius is silent by the curb.

I round the corner next to the last house on the dead-end street and find myself at the edge of a greenbelt shaded with tall, dense oak trees. This is more like it.

Using the foliage as cover, I make my way to the back patio of the house where I suspect my father is situated according to my app.

My heart nearly stops when the screen door flings open. I leap backward and press my back against the nearest tree trunk to stay out of sight. I see a plump woman with short blonde hair in a summer dress bursting out of the house, laughing and moving as if someone's chasing her. Then my father rushes out of the door and envelops the woman in his arms from behind, kissing the side of her neck.

"Oh, Dickie, you're such a bad boy," the woman coos in a profoundly affectionate voice.

Dickie? My father's name is Robert. He is a fifty-nine years old businessman. How dare she call him Dickie?

What I'm witnessing crumbles my entire world. My father is my hero and my idol. He is an honest, hardworking man who lives for his family. He never laid a hand on my mother or any of his children. I can count on one hand how many times he raised his voice at us. He is a poster child, husband, and father. Yet I'm seeing him frolicking around with another woman like I've never seen him behave before. He seems so happy, free, and careless.

I feel as if I'm sinking into the earth. I can't breathe, yet a sickening desire keeps my eyes on the couple. They touch and kiss, then my father slips his hand into the woman's dress and gropes her right breast. That's too much for my eyes to behold. I'll be sick. I have to get out of here.

As I turn, I lock eyes with an elderly lady who is staring at me through a screened window in the house next to me.

"Who are you?" she shrieks, and her voice prompts me to run before I'm discovered. Retracing my steps, I sprint to the street and slam against the white Prius driving by slowly. I rip the door open and jump inside.

"Is everything okay?" The driver eyes me, bewildered. "I thought you weren't coming back."

I wipe my forehead with the back of my hand, lock the door, and scoot to the middle of the back seat. "Everything is peachy. I need you to take me back to San Marcos, please."

The guy sweeps his eyes over the street behind him, as if looking for a clue, then he turns forward and drives away.

I'm hot. I'm sweaty. I'm heartbroken. I take a bottled water from the cooler at my feet and drink it with gusto.

I always thought the reason I could never find a man I wanted to marry was because nobody could measure up to my father. But he is a cheat and a liar! Suddenly, having a bastard brother doesn't seem so far-fetched. He was young when he married my mother, but I always thought he was content with his life. He never seemed regretful of missing out on the fun other young men had the privilege to enjoy. Was this woman his first mistress? Were there any others? How many more brothers and sisters do I have that I don't know about? And the biggest question remains: Does my mother know about his infidelity?

A text comes in from Anaya. We are at the ME's office. Meredith put up a hell of a fight. Has over half a dozen defensive wounds just like Linda. What time will you be back?

I take a moment to push my personal problems to the side and focus on the murder investigation. I close my eyes and take a few breaths.

In 10 min. I'll see u in a bit, I text back.

After my Uber driver drops me off at the hospital, I vape for a few minutes to buy time to organize my thoughts. If I tell my mother what I know, my parents might get divorced. If I don't tell her, then I'm an accomplice to my father's crimes. I try to figure out what I would want if I were in my mother's shoes. But it's hard to identify with her because I've never been married and never had children. I can't even consider the situation unbiasedly because, at this moment, I condemn all men in the world to hell for one man's crime.

20

Brestler and Reed have been waiting for me at the morgue, where a forensic medical examiner named Dr. Julia Kendrick did the autopsy on Meredith Falcone, and now she is running her preliminary findings by us. Blood, saliva, fiber, and hair samples found on the victim's clothes and body were bagged and sent to the lab for analysis. I learned the doctor had also combed the deceased's hair and scrapped her fingernails for trace evidence, and swabbed for vaginal fluid, although Meredith wasn't sexually assaulted.

The cause of death was severe blood loss and loss of function of several essential organs due to seventeen knife-inflicted stab wounds. The young mother was a fighter. She had tried to block the blade with her arms and sustained eight defensive wounds by doing so. Two of those cuts were long and deep gashes, and I could only imagine the pain and hopelessness she must have felt during the attack. As I look down at the dead girl's body, a profound sadness comes over me. No young child should ever have to bury her mother.

Anaya is intensely studying the autopsy report of the former victim, Linda Osborne, as she stands next to me, holding a beige folder in her hand.

Brestler is on the phone with the chief a few feet away from us, facing the corner. I overhear statements like, "It seems like it, sir." And "I'll brief you soon."

As part of a special operations team, we are not permitted to discuss details about our investigation in front of an unauthorized person, so we refrain from sharing theories for the time being. We are only here to collect as much information as possible for future analysis.

I'm hungry, and my stomach gives a loud growl. I try to mask it by turning to the ME with a question. "What's your professional opinion about the killer's MO? Do you think we are dealing with the same guy who killed Linda Osborne a few weeks ago?"

The lady in the white coat across the table from me looks nothing like how I imagine a forensic pathologist to look like. She is a beautiful seasoned woman with a slim, tall frame and delicately tied-up blonde hair. Her smooth skin and subtle makeup grant her an air of elegance. She carries herself confidently, a person in charge. She rather gives off the impression of being more a CEO or college professor than someone who cuts up people for a living. Yet, she speaks softly. Her voice is soothing. Following her notes, she tells us about her findings as airily as if she were sharing her favorite recipe with us.

My profiling mode turns on. I assume that the doctor grew up in a wealthy, Orange County family. Her parents' primary focus from an early age—maybe as early as kindergarten—was her education and future career path. By the time she was accepted into college, there was no question about her becoming a doctor. Spending four years on campus, she was exposed to new ideologies and progressive world views that altered her compliant and dutiful demeanor. She rebelled against her parents by choosing pathology over a career as a surgeon. But she wouldn't stray far from the original plan because she understood the hard work and dedication needed to get this far. Her yearning for her parents' approval has never ebbed.

If she has children, they must be older now—college-aged. I wonder if she let her kids carelessly enjoy their childhood or followed her parents' example and set her children on a specific path early on too?

Dr. Kendrick pulls off the gloves with her manicured long fingers and slips them into her pocket. "I didn't do Linda Osborne's autopsy, but I read the report. The distinctive way of committing the crime in both cases is eerily similar, almost identical. It strikes me as somewhat odd."

She speaks without emotion in a low monotone voice. No matter how hard I try, I can't picture this delicate woman wearing a blood-spattered safety mask, cutting through the bone and flesh of a dead body.

"Serial killers tend to stick to specific methods," Anaya says, reinserting herself into the conversation. "They commit their crimes using the techniques that work for them. We typically only see a change in a serial killer's MO after the media foolishly releases a piece of detailed information about the investigation, inadvertently warning the perpetrator that he is leaving a trail for the police to follow."

"Like the Southriver Rapist in Ventura." I may not be a seasoned homicide detective, but I've done my homework. "He dumped his victims by the side of remote dirt roads. When he learned about the pieces of fibers he left on his victims in the media, he started dumping the bodies into the river to wash away any trace evidence."

Dr. Kendrick rubs her hands with lotion. "That's entirely correct. Serial killers hunt on familiar ground and use methods they are confident in. However, in these two homicide cases, the bodies were positioned in the exact same way, both victims stabbed the exact same number of times, in the exact same location, which is their kitchen. It's almost . . . ritual-like."

I lock eyes with Anaya. Her suspicion of us hunting a copycat killer who tries to pin his murders on other killers is building credence. Or are we fitting facts to fit our theory?

Brestler returns to the table. "Chief wants us to stay here for a few days and investigate. You okay with that?" He poses his question straight at me.

"Yep. Doug is away for a realtor conference all weekend. There's nothing but an empty house for me at home."

Brestler doesn't ask Anaya if she was okay with staying. Single people are naturally assumed to have more free time and flexible schedules. Still, Anaya shows no signs of being offended.

Detective Brown pushes his way into the room through the swinging double door.

"Julia," he calls out to the ME.

"David," she acknowledges him.

The detective remains by the door, keeping one panel from slamming shut. "If you guys are done here, I can take you to the captain's office."

"We appreciate it, thank you," says Brestler.

"I'll make a copy for you," Dr. Kendrick says, lifting the autopsy report. "The toxicology and the analysis on the trace evidence may take a week or more."

We don't shake hands. Dr. Kendrick doesn't touch people without gloves. She's germophobic.

"At first, I thought she refused to shake my hand because I'm black," Anaya whispers in my ear as we follow Detective Brown out of the building.

"Did you experience any racial discrimination in England?"

"No, but before I moved here, I was under the illusion that rich, white people were all racist in America."

"What would give you that impression?"

Anaya shrugs. "I don't know. Movies. The media."

It wasn't the time or the place to go into a debate about discrimination, so I merely touched her arm to acknowledge what she said and then turned to Brestler. If I don't get a chance to visit my mother this weekend to find out the truth, then I might as well do the best I can with this investigation.

"I'd like to go to the gentlemen's club and talk to the owner and other dancers who knew Meredith. Maybe they know a guy who was obsessed with her or had a beef with her. I'd also like to interview Meredith's parents."

Brestler takes a sharp inhale, then he leans closer to me "It's not normal procedure for FBI agents to conduct those interviews. We haven't announced our theory of a serial killer in action yet. I don't want to step on any toes here. I know you were a detective before you joined the Bureau, so I'm sure you understand how sensitive local law enforcement can be about jurisdiction."

"I understand, sir. Although I worked cybercrimes, I'm used to collaborating with other agencies," I correct him. "That's why we were so efficient."

Brestler smiles at me warmly. "Noted."

I wait until he's done scratching his day-old facial hair and makes a decision. "How about you hint a few details about our investigation to Detective Brown to make him feel included, then your request of joining him for a visit to the strip bar won't raise any eyebrows?"

"That sounds doable, sir. Thank you."

Brestler beckons me closer. "Remember. Lead the horse to water, but let him drink on his own."

21

The Black Panther Gentlemen's Club offers a wide variety of cultures from around the globe. The owner is a Russian that moved to California ten years ago when he was twenty-seven-years old from a small town called Leskolovoner, near Saint Petersburg. The few girls on stage and displayed on lit billboards around the walls are mostly Hispanic. The head of security is from Durban, a coastal city in South Africa, and the bartender is American-Canadian who, according to the owner, has lived his entire life in southern California.

Back in the captain's office, I suggested to Detective Brown that we start our investigation at Meredith's workplace. He said he was already on his way to the club, and I was welcome to join him. Brestler and Reed remained at San Marcos PD to help set up a control center for the investigating team.

According to the owner of this "gentleman's" club, Mr. Anatoly, it's too early in the day for business, and most of the girls aren't expected in until later. I feel guilty for derailing Brown's investigation by missing the crucial detail about the business hours being busier in the evening at a place like this. We should have gone to Meredith's parents first, but I was too focused on finding a disgruntled customer that might have killed the young girl that would disprove our copycat serial-killer theory. The mere thought of having a calculating and intelligent criminal at large was chilling me to the bone.

But Brown asks Anatoly to round up the girls for a voluntary interview to help the police identify anyone who may have had a reason to harm their friend, Meredith. The request doesn't sit well with the owner, I notice. He looks more annoyed than heartbroken over the dancer's death. He talks about Meredith as if she were merely a piece of valuable merchandise stolen from him. Despite his annoyance, Anatoly retires to his office to make the calls.

As Brown and I are left to wait between the bar and the stage, I use my time to get a better feel for the place and what might have prompted a young mother, like Meredith, to choose this line of work. On center stage, two girls are wrapping their scantily clad bodies around the poles, performing for a handful of men nursing their drinks and gawking at the dancers. A single waitress is perched on a bar stool with her legs crossed, giggling at the bartender, undisturbed by the police presence.

The enormous room has no windows or clocks to warn its customers about the passing of time. Blinded by neon lights and hypnotized by beautiful naked girls, a man could easily lose track of time here. I wonder how many marriages have been ruined or saved by this establishment. How many strip bars has Doug visited during our relationship?

Anatoly returns from his office. He walks with a slight limp and looks like someone my mother would call a *slimeball*. His overly tanned and skinny body is mostly covered with black jeans, a white V-neck t-shirt, and a black leather vest. He seems to be obsessively trying to look younger. He's had considerable plastic surgery to his face that stands out from his blemished and sagging neck. Both his arms are a canvas of elaborate tattoos, the images undistinguishable. His nose is pierced with golden jewels as if he belongs to an ancient African tribe. And every time he moves his hands, a wide array of gold bangles jingles on his wrists.

He salutes us. "I've done what I can, but I don't expect much success. At the sight of cops, these girls turn and run, you know what I'm saying?"

"Was the same bartender working here Wednesday night?" Brown asks.

Anatoly plays with his chin hair as he turns to check the identity of the person behind the bar. "Liam? No, he wasn't, but that's Portia with him. She is, I mean was, Meredith's closest friend here," he says, turning a thick golden ring on his finger. "Another girl, Lyric, was close to her too, but she isn't working tonight."

"Do you have security cameras?" I ask, pointing at the black orb mounted on the ceiling.

Anatoly knits his eyebrows tightly as he measures me up. "Yeah, of course. But you'll need a warrant to get the tapes. Sorry, sweetheart, nothing personal but I've been burned by law enforcement too many times. I've learned my lesson, you know what I'm saying?"

I step forward with a stern expression. "I'm Special Agent Vicky Collins with the FBI, you may address me as ma'am, or Agent Collins."

Anatoly quickly throws his hands in the air. "A kitty with claws, I love it!"

Detective Brown steps between us before the situation escalates. I follow his lead and head to the bar to talk to Portia, a bitter taste in my mouth. Why is it okay for men to engage in cockfights while women are always told to let it go?

During the short interview with Portia, I learn that she is a single mom with a four-year-old boy. As we talk, she frequently reminds us that she is only dancing for the money so she can save up for college. I don't judge her. I've never been in her shoes.

We're told that Meredith didn't have any known enemies and only a couple of harmless guys had made advances on her in the past year, but according to Portia, that's not unusual in a place like this. A few girls earn a little extra cash on the side with sugar daddies too. The girls would accept gifts and money from older men, but Meredith wasn't one of them.

Brown takes the first names of the frequent customers who showed a particular interest in Meredith because that's all men give out around here. Anatoly can't verify the girl's list. He says he doesn't get involved with his employees' personal lives.

Then we tell Portia about Meredith's death, saving her from the brutal details. Brown and I are standing in silence as she cries, cuddled in the bartender's arms.

Portia pleads for us to catch the killer and make sure he's punished. She seems genuine as she dabs at her tearing eyes with a napkin. When I ask her if she remembers anything unusual from the past few weeks, she recalls an incident that happened to her and Monique, Meredith's stage name, back in May. They went to grab a drink at a bar near the beach after work one night—Portia can't remember which one—while Portia was outside for a smoke, Meredith met a guy who caught her eye, but when she jokingly called him gay for not responding to her flirting, the man exploded in a fit of rage. Meredith was so shocked and scared, that she left, grabbing Portia on the way. She spent the night at her parents' house because she didn't want to be alone.

That would have been an excellent lead to start with, but Portia didn't know the name of the guy or have a description of him. She said Monique only called him good-looking. I guess it's not surprising that Portia can't recall any details about the perp. That night must have been one of many.

I make a note to remind myself to ask Meredith's parents about the incident. If she did stay at her parents' house the night of the incident, she might have shared more details about the guy with them.

The bartender, Liam, isn't much help. He's been working at the club for only a few months, and although he knew "Monique," he didn't have a relationship with her apart from being work colleagues. Brown doesn't find his statement suspicious, and I trust his guts on this one. He's been a homicide detective for the San Diego County Sheriff's Department for twelve years.

There's not much else we learn here and, as Anatoly foretold, not a single girl shows up to talk to us.

Brown hands his card to the Russian owner and asks him to have Lyric call him as soon as possible.

"We need to get a court order to obtain the security video," Brown says as we get into his car. "Can you believe what that girl said? She's only working here to earn money for college. What a truckload of bull."

I grimace and refrain from commenting. I knew girls from high school who became pregnant and the baby daddy took off. If a young single mom has no parents or family to support her, then doors close on her real fast. Not many businesses are eager to employ a high-school dropout who misses a significant number of days at work because she has no one to look after her baby. I also knew girls whose parents and family supported them through teenage pregnancy. They managed to finish school, go to college, and attain respectable jobs. Judging is easy to do, but we shouldn't do it until we've lived two lives.

As I secure my seatbelt, I notice a missed call from an unidentified number and the notification icon for a voice mail on the screen of my phone. I open the voicemail message: it's from the deputy warden of the Larry P. Smith Correctional Facility.

"Agent Collins, this is Matt Zielinski from Smith's. I'm sorry to bother you. I heard about the interview, or I should say the lack of it, you conducted with inmate Paul Gooden. He'd like to apologize for his behavior and has some information to share with you . . . useful information this time, I understand. Please come back and visit us at your convenience."

After all the recent dead ends during my investigations, this new development is a breath of fresh air. Once I'm able to break away from here to visit my mother in Temecula, I'll certainly swing by the prison to see Gooden. That trip will also allow me to stop by Beaumont and speak with Barbara Sullivan, Blake's aunt, as well.

The overwhelming number of tasks, vying for priority, mentally weigh me down. I feel a decade older. Worn and tired. In my life, when it rains, it pours.

Brown talks to his wife on the phone on the way to the Falcone family home, and I use the time to check Doug's Instagram posts. After looking at half a dozen pictures and short videos commemorating his timeline, I feel as if I participated in the event. He appears to be happier than I've ever felt in my life. He is dressed elegantly, borderline flamboyant. He is surrounded by thriving and ambitious people. He makes a fortune selling properties people bought or built with their blood and sweat; yet, he is glorified for it.

I'm surrounded by the scum of the earth, death, and sadness. I make less money bringing justice to families than Doug does selling houses. As a part of the law-enforcement community, I'm disliked by default, and nobody thinks they need us until they do. We get to be heroes for our fifteen minutes of fame. Then it's over, and we are forgotten once again.

Where is the justice in that?

22

The Falcone house is a typical track home on a napkin-sized piece of land in a suburban area of San Marcos, and a fifteen-minute drive from Meredith's apartment. It's a two-story, two-car garage home painted in an HOA-approved pastel color with a matching tile roof. In the front yard, the fronds of tall queen palms sway in the warm afternoon breeze, casting elongated animated shadows onto the two SUVs on the driveway.

A sheriff deputy's cruiser parked by the sidewalk is radiating heat from the summer sun. Brown steers his black Camaro behind it and turns off the engine. I'm relieved to learn that they have already informed the parents about Meredith's death, so I don't have to witness their first reaction to hearing about losing their daughter. I don't do well in the company of crying people.

The Falcones managed a local nursery for over twenty-five years until their older son took over the business three years ago. The son has been interviewed and has an alibi for the murder. He was home with his wife and three-year-old daughter. The Falcones' younger son is enlisted in the Navy and is currently stationed in

Souda Bay, Crete. Other than that, there is scant information in the preliminary report.

A short, plump female officer opens the front door for us. "Mr. Falcone is in the living room. Mrs. Falcone is on medication. She's sleeping in the bedroom," she informs us as we pass through the threshold.

The moment we step inside, we encounter an overwhelming number of religious relics and paintings in the house. As I advance deeper into the home, images of Jesus crucified on a cross gaze down at me from every direction. I feel as if He is penetrating my soul, seeing my deepest secrets. I always considered one's need for extreme displays of faith as a means to repent for past sins. For what sins are the Falcones repenting?

The living room is a big bright space overstuffed with furniture and decoration. Mr. Falcone is sitting alone on the couch, torn with grief. He is a short white male with a shiny bald head except for a belt of brown hair around the back of his head. A bushy dark mustache perched over his upper lip is dripping with tears.

"Mr. Falcone," calls out the sheriff's deputy. "Detective David Brown from the San Diego County's Sheriff Department and Special Agent Vicky Collins with the FBI are here to speak with you."

The grieving father reaches for his glasses on the table, puts them on, and looks at me. "The FBI?"

Since he has engaged with me and, well, it's true men tend to react more to female empathy, I sit beside him and take the lead. "Please accept my deepest condolences. I'm truly sorry for your loss."

"Thank you," the man says, dabbing at his eyes underneath his glasses with a Kleenex.

"I know that the news is still fresh, and I can only imagine the pain you are going through right now, but we have a few questions regarding your daughter's whereabouts and friends. We'd deeply appreciate it if you could help us."

The man purses his lips, bobbing his head slightly. Agony is written all over his face. There is no doubt in my mind that the death of his daughter killed a part of him.

"Earlier today, Detective Brown and I talked to one of Meredith's colleagues at the Black Panther, and she mentioned an alarming event that took place sometime back in May. The story we heard was that your daughter had a falling out with a stranger at a bar. Meredith's friend couldn't tell us the name of the establishment or when exactly the incident occurred, but it was serious enough for Meredith to fear for her safety. We were told that on that particular night, she drove here and stayed the night. Do you recall any of this?"

The man looks at me with glossy eyes like marbles, long and silent, as if ransacking his brain for that specific memory. "Yes, I do remember that night. Merri showed up at the house around four in the morning. I remember because she almost gave me a heart attack with her knocking. She was rattled and definitely scared. She thought someone was following her, but I didn't see anybody on the street."

"Did she perhaps give you a description of the person or the car that followed her?"

Mr. Falcone shakes his head, then breaks into a fit of crying. "I should have let her move back home. She asked for my help, but I said it was time for her to stand on her own two feet."

I put my hand on the man's back, exchanging silent glances with Brown, who was sitting on the recliner underneath a white statue of Jesus with open arms, showing the wounds from the crucifixion on his palms.

"This isn't your fault, Mr. Falcone. We do all that we can to protect the ones we love, but sometimes, no matter what we do, terrible things happen," I say, handing him a clean tissue from the box on the table.

Mr. Falcone sniffles and blows his nose. "She was a good girl, you know? 'A's and 'B's all throughout high school. She ran track and played volleyball. Then she met that boy, that good-for-nothing hooligan, Nikko Gonzalez. Everything went to hell after that."

"Mr. Gonzalez is the father of Meredith's daughter, Jessica," Brown informs me.

"Oh, God, how do we tell Jess that her mommy has gone to heaven?" Mr. Falcone cries out. "Maybe if I was nicer to Nikko, they would've stayed together. Maybe if we had welcomed him into the family, he would've treated my sweet Merri better." He looks up at me with tearful eyes. "He broke her heart, you know? She was never the same after their breakup. She spent the rest of her life trying to prove to herself that she was worthy of love. That's why she danced. She wanted the attention, you know?"

I glance up at the face of Jesus. I was raised Catholic, but I haven't been to church since I left home. I remember the words of the priest from Susie's funeral. That's all I'm able to offer to this grieving father at the moment. "God is with her, Mr. Falcone. God loves your daughter. I'm sure she is in a better place right now."

His swollen, red fingers squeeze my hand. "Thank you," Mr. Falcone whispers. "Thank you for saying that."

The broken man looks somewhat composed now and focused.

"I want you to catch the bastard that did this to my daughter." Mr. Falcone makes his point by looking at each one of us in the eyes.

"We'll do everything we can to apprehend the person responsible," promises Brown.

"Mr. Falcone," I ask. "Do you suspect Mr. Gonzales of hurting your daughter?"

The man sighs. "I don't know. He hasn't been a part of her life these past ten years, not since Jessica was born. That scumbag doesn't even pay child support."

"Would he benefit somehow from the death of your daughter?"

My words sink in too fast. A ripple of apprehension runs down the man's face, and his head drops into his hands again. He shakes his head no and starts rolling a rosary between his fingers as tears gather in his eyes. "I should have let her move back home."

His mind seems to slip in and out of focus. I give him a minute to gather himself, then continue, "Did your daughter share any details about the man that harassed her in the bar back in May?"

"Oh, yeah—" He's with us once again. "Erm, no, she didn't. I'm sorry. I wish she had. It was very early in the morning. We didn't talk much. She went to bed, and I did the same." Every word he utters seems to pain him. Maybe it's better if I never have children.

"Do you think Meredith talked to your wife about that night?" Brown asks.

Mr. Falcone scratches his forehead. He wants to help us, but it's evident he wants to be left alone with his grieving.

"I don't think so. Merri was up early, grabbed Jessica, and left. She even left her leather jacket she wore that night. She said the guy spat on it and she didn't want it anymore."

I don't think I heard him right. My eyes snap to Brown. His face is lit with excitement.

"Do you still have the jacket in your possession?" I repeat the question to confirm what I heard.

"Yes. My wife hung it in Merri's closet. We kept forgetting to give it to her, and Merri never asked for it back."

"Sir, may we have that jacket?"

"Certainly." Mr. Falcone presses down on his thighs to push himself up. "Let me get if for you."

Meredith's room is now Jessica's room. The ten-year-old girl lies on the bed playing with her phone, a pair of AirPods poking from her ears. She must be listening to music because our intrusion doesn't alarm her.

Her grandpa touches her ankle. The girl jumps. "What the hell? You scared the shit out of me!"

"Watch your mouth, Jess!" Mr. Falcone snaps, blushing. "She has a little behavior problem," he tells us in a mere whisper.

"Whatever," the girl groans and rolls to her other side.

A moment of uncomfortable silence follows as Mr. Falcone removes a rusty-red leather jacket from the closet. Brown leans in to take the curved metal head of the hanger from him. A deputy is right behind us with an oversized evidence bag, and Brown carefully lowers the garment into it.

We thank Mr. Falcone for his cooperation and return to the car.

"Do you think the lab rats will have enough saliva to establish a DNA profile?" Brown asks.

"I don't know, but if they do, we're nailing this son of a bitch."

23

Brestler books rooms for us at the Fairfield Inn in the heart of San Marcos, not far from the crime scene. Our unit is on a tight budget, so Anaya and I volunteer to share a room.

After we check in, I let Anaya settle in the room first. I take a seat on a leather loveseat near the reception to stay out of the heat and call Doug to hear how the convention is going. He answers his phone after the second ring, which takes me by surprise. He says he's in his room. The TV chatter in the background verifies his story.

"Are you going out?" I ask unnecessarily. Of course, he's going out! Why do I even ask?

"Not tonight, I'm spent. Oh man, Vicky, today was amazing," he gushes. "We had over two hundred people in the room. Many of them were standing in the back because we didn't have enough chairs. They were all there to hear me talk about how I built my social-media platform for business. It was unbelievable! Freaking mind-blowing!"

"I'm so proud of you, Doug. Look how far you've come."

"I couldn't have done it without you. I owe you big time, Vic. Don't ever forget that."

Ethan calls me Vic, so it's strange to hear it from Doug.

"I only assisted. You did the heavy lifting."

Doug laughs heartily. "Oh, Vicky, I miss you. I wish you were here to see all those people. I nailed it. I n.a.i.l.e.d. it!"

"I knew you would."

"Enough about me. Are you back home?"

"No," I sigh. "I'm stuck in San Marcos. We got a break, so we might have a lead. If not, I'll be here for a while."

"No worries. Hey, babe, I gotta go. Ethan ordered us room service, and the waiter is at the door. We're too tired to go out to eat."

"Sounds lovely. Enjoy. I'll see you back home."

My loneliness and heartache keep me sitting for a long time. As strange as it sounds, I want to be with Doug in that hotel room, ordering room service. I imagine putting on a soft white bathrobe and lying on the bed with my boyfriend, watching Impractical Jokers on TruTV. We'd eat steak and wash our dinner down with champagne. I want Doug to make love to me and afterward get in the shower with me. I want to laugh and act silly. I want to let loose and enjoy our relationship. I want to live my life a little. But that's not happening tonight. Duty calls.

Anaya is in the bathroom when I enter the room. I hear water pelting against the tile. She is singing. I wish I knew what perked her up. I could use some of the same medicine.

I sit down at the end of the bed and turn on the TV. I flip through the channels, but nothing catches my interest.

"Oh, you're back. Good," Anaya calls out. "You want to grab some chow with Brestler and me?"

She says this as if they were a couple.

"Sure. Why not?" I attempt to smile.

Anaya rolls her wet hair into a towel turban and sits beside me. "What's wrong? I thought you'd be happy about the saliva sample."

"I am. It's . . . nothing, really. It's just—" I take a deep breath. "I talked to Doug. He's up in Irvine with Ethan at a realtor convention. He's one of the keynote speakers. It's a big moment for him, and I'm missing it, as always."

Anaya tosses her arm over me. "Then drive up there and surprise him!"

"It's over an hour's drive."

"Who cares? That's nothing." Anaya grabs her phone from the nightstand and checks traffic on Google Maps. "Look, it's smooth sailing."

Gazing at the digital map, I let the idea marinate for a second. I've never surprised Doug before, but maybe it's the spice we need in our relationship. Spontaneity.

"Do you think I should?"

"Look, Vicky. You work hard. You are dedicated to the Bureau, but don't let your work consume your life. It's only a job. Go! See Doug."

A rush of excitement bubbles up inside me. "I'll be back first thing in the morning."

Anaya waves her hand back. "We can hold down the fort until you get back. The girl is dead and there's nothing we can do to bring her back."

I jump up from the bed and start peeling off my clothes to get in the shower. "But if that girl, Lyric, calls from the Black Panther, I want to know about it! Also, if you hear anything from the lab—"

"It's late. We won't hear anything new till morning," she interrupts my babbling. "But if there's any new development, I'll call you right away. I promise."

Guilt, mixed with anticipation, coils inside me as I wash up. I can't stop convincing myself that this is a bad idea. But I'm on a roll, so let's go.

Anaya lends me her car, and I'm on the road by 21:30.

The traffic has died down, as Anaya predicated, and I practically fly on the freeway to Irvine.

I stop at a 7-11 to pick up a bottle of champagne, then continue on to Doug's hotel.

It takes a little persuasion and FBI badge power to persuade the concierge to give me a key to Doug's room.

When I open the door, the first thing I notice is the sweet fragrance of burning candles, and my heart begins to race at once. I lower the bottle of champagne in my hand and move toward the flickering light cast on the wall by the candles.

An eruption of sexual moaning stops my heart. I'm paralyzed. My feet won't move. I want to run away before I see something that can't be unseen, but my curiosity won't let me.

I set the bottle on a table by the bathroom door, touch my Glock to make sure I have it with me and flip on the light switch. I round the corner quickly to get a view of the bed. If one of those bitches from Doug's Instagram posts is in bed with him, I swear to God, I'll claw the bimbo's eyes out!

The brightness from the overhead lights spills onto two mounds beneath white sheets on the bed.

"Doug!" I shudder at the weakness of my voice that's not more than a yelp.

The bodies freeze, pretending not to be there.

"Doug?" I call out, somewhat more confident.

My nose twitches and tears are beginning to well in my eyes.

The sheet lifts and Doug's tousled head emerges. "What are you doing here?"

His face is void of color, completely white. His pale lips quiver. I think he's shaking, but it might be me.

"Who is under the blanket?" I ask breathlessly.

"It's nobody," Doug whispers.

I pull out my gun, grasping it with both hands, and level it at my boyfriend's head.

"Who the fuck is under the blanket, Doug?" I shout, trembling with anger.

The cover slowly slips down. At the sight of the person that my eyes behold, my knees buckle, and my finger arches over the trigger.

It's Ethan. It's butt-naked, fucking Ethan. In bed with my boyfriend.

24

The strength is draining from my arms as I aim my gun with both hands at Doug's heart, my finger releasing off the trigger. Doug puts his hand up as a barricade to protect himself. My eyes go in and out of focus of his white palm. I make out every line and ridge running down from his fingers. His lifeline is short and ends with a cluster of downward branching lines, like tassels. I know the patterns on Doug's palm well. I harbor sweet memories of nights when we drank and laughed, reading each other's fortune from the palms of our hands. Neither of us believed in that foolish hocus-pocus, but it was fun to make up stories about how our lives might turn out or how they would end. Based on Doug's short lifeline, he was destined to die at a relatively young age. Maybe in a car accident or from an unknown virus that doctors wouldn't be able to identify. I'd be by his bedside, supporting him through the hardship because this is who I am: a loyal dog.

We no longer have to speculate about the future. Doug's future is here. He will die at a young age from a gunshot wound to the chest.

As the past and present mangle in my mind, I become disoriented, having an out-of-body experience. My trigger finger cramps and I lose control of it. My mind is telling me to turn and run, but a mixture of hate and disgust is burning inside me. It's too painful to move.

Doug rolls onto his knees, keeping his hand up. "Vicky, please put the gun down," he says in a voice designed to soothe.

My lying-piece-of-shit boyfriend's effort to defuse the situation does not work on me. I'm dumbfounded and stark-raving mad from this betrayal. I've never felt so humiliated and hurt in my entire life. I find myself stooping so low emotionally that I wish it were one of his lady friends from the office he was screwing—or even three of them. But not another man. Not Ethan.

Why? The question bounces around in my skull. Why?

"It's not what it seems." Doug attempts to defuse the tension in the room, but I can't take him seriously with his nipples poking at me. "I can explain."

I blink to get rid of the tears in my eyes and regain my vision. "Oh, please do explain. I'd love to hear you talk yourself out of this one."

"I'm not gay," Ethan says as if it was his turn to talk.

My jaws clench. "Nobody asked you!" I can't even look at him or acknowledge his presence in the room. He is—*was*—my friend. He kissed me only yesterday. How stupid I am for not recognizing his romantic advances toward me as an act—a ploy to detach me emotionally from my boyfriend, so Ethan can have him to himself.

Ethan is a monster! He's destroyed everything Doug and I have built for the past decade. If my father were here

. . . Why am I bringing my father into this? He is another lying, cheating, sack of shit.

There is no winning for women in a relationship.

If we stay at home to raise children and keep the household and get a little too comfortable and fat in the process, then we're deemed as money-sucking leeches who also lost their sex appeal. So, men think it's okay to cheat to feel the excitement again.

If we work and let nannies raise our children and keep our home in order, then we're condemned for not caring enough about our husbands and kids. So, men think it's okay to cheat to get more attention.

If we make more money than our husband, then we are accused of being patronizing. So, men think it's okay to cheat to feel better about themselves.

If we make less, then we're criticized for not earning more, and on, and on, and on. There is no escaping this catch-22.

I'm not surprised everybody is on pills in this country.

Doug lowers his head and steals a glance at his friend, huddling underneath the blanket next to him, then looks back at me. "Please, put the gun down, and we can talk," he orders me like I work for him; as if I were a homicidal maniac who can't be trusted with a weapon. I'm a trained FBI agent, for Christ's sake!

I turn the Glock sideways, waving it up and down toward him. "What? This? You think I can't control myself? You think I'd shoot your sorry ass and ruin my life? For what? For you?" I aim the gun at the center of his chest again, my eyes widening into a crazy gaze because it feels empowering to do so.

I've done everything he's ever asked of me. I've supported him through school, his career, his ups and downs. I gave him my heart. I stripped my soul naked in front of him. I allowed him to get close to me, to see me vulnerable, and he took advantage of my trust.

Doug sits back on his heels. "May I get dressed at least?"

I marvel at the transformation his face has gone through in the past few minutes, turning from white to bright red.

He was so eager to prance around naked in bed with another man, he shouldn't worry about being exposed now. He never has a problem with walking around at home with his cock hanging out.

If I had the balls, I'd force him to parade naked down the hotel hallway for all to see. Isn't that what he likes? To be the center of attention? To be looked at? Admired? I want him to feel as naked and humiliated as I do.

Despite my nasty words and thoughts, I'm not a monster. I'm an FBI agent. I'm the keeper of the law. I holster my gun and nod at Doug, indicating that he has my permission to put on his clothes. Having a loaded gun in your hand is empowering. Not pulling the trigger—even more so.

Doug swallows his next words, struggling to stay mute. Then he signals to Ethan, and they both slip out of bed, barefooted and nude. I step into the bathroom to spare myself the sight.

I lock the door behind me, mourning my decade of trust I had in my boyfriend. I should have never let him get close to me. I was just as happy living alone before I met him.

I wash my face with cold water, soak a hand towel in the sink, and scrub off my makeup. My stubborn mascara leaves traces of black around my eyes, turning me into an evil villain. Who am I kidding? I loved Doug, and I still do. He is my best friend. My lover. He is the one who knows more about me than anyone else in this wretched world.

But it's over now. Things will never be the same between us. Losing him is like losing a limb. I should have never driven here. It would have been better if I'd never found out the truth.

My chest violently begins to shake, and I sit down on the edge of the bathtub and cry. What hurts the most is the realization that my boyfriend cared so little for me that he was able to use me as an accessory, a prop for his social life to hide his true identity.

I rub my face with both hands, spreading salty tears around my face. Then I laugh out loud in desperation. It's almost comical how this revelation brings other details about my relationship with Doug into focus. Tonight's episode was the missing puzzle piece to finally put the whole picture together. There was always a lingering suspicion in the back of my mind that Doug was different. He has a borderline feminine obsession with his appearances—his hair, nails, and clothes always have to be perfect. Before he would touch me, he needed a few drinks and a bedroom clothed in darkness. I noticed those things. I contributed his shyness and lack of interest in sex to a difficult upbringing. I believed his passage from child to adult wasn't paved with healthy sexual experiences and left him insecure in his own body.

In light of recent events, I have a new theory. Doug's two older brothers may have exposed him to inappropriate adult content early in his youth, leading him down a path of sexual deviance. Or maybe he was born this way, but his parents wouldn't accept a gay son, so he learned to conceal his feelings as a child by any means necessary—even if it meant destroying someone else's life.

I drink water from the faucet to put a stop to my speculating. My profiling has been off lately, and I don't feel confident about my theories. I was utterly wrong about Meredith's background, and my own boyfriend has been leading me on for years.

If I knew Doug's family, I could investigate his childhood and find out what led him to lie about who he really is, but I've never met any of them. Doug was estranged from his family way before I met him. I only have the childhood stories he shared with me—if they were real at all.

A series of gentle knocks raps on the door. "Are you okay in there?"

"No, I'm not fucking okay, Doug!" I yell.

No answer.

I hear receding footsteps.

"Fuck!" I scream, punching the tile on the wall. The pain comes fast and hard. I put my throbbing knuckles under a cold stream of water. I take a few deep breaths and dry my hands and face with a towel.

By the time I muster the courage to exit the bathroom to face Doug and Ethan, I feel empty. The life has been sucked out of me.

Doug is standing by the window, gazing at the lit-up sparkling pool on the ground floor.

Ethan is leaning against the desk, his arms folded.

I can't even look at them. I set my gaze on the carpet and start chewing the inside of my mouth.

"Vic—" Ethan begins, but I stop him right here.

"I need to talk to Doug alone," I say as maturely as I can manage.

Ethan runs his hand down his bushy beard and pushes away from the desk. "I understand."

When the room's door shuts behind me, I shudder.

"How long has this been going on?"

Doug can't look me in the eyes either. We both keep glancing at each other, then snap our eyes away, searching for something neutral to look at.

"Nothing is going on Vicky. I promise."

"I don't need more lies. I want to hear the truth."

"I'm telling you the truth. I don't know what happened tonight. Honestly. We got back to the room after the convention, high on adrenaline and drunk. It was . . . well . . . we were . . . I don't know. The whole thing seems surreal."

I don't respond. Doug needs to sweat this one out without my help.

"We had some drinks. I ordered pay-per-view. It was stupid."

"You watched porn with your best friend?"

Doug's shoulder slump. I don't see the successful businessman in him anymore. He's a lost little boy, desperate for approval.

"It started out as a guy thing. I don't know . . . Please don't make me say it out loud."

I scoff. "Oh, you want me to make it easier on you? If you think it's tough to talk about, guess how I felt seeing it?"

Doug looks at me. His eyes are bloodshot. His hands are shaking.

There is nothing else to talk about. There is no point in stretching out this heartbreaking and humiliating conversation for either of us. I reach for my purse lying on the floor where I dropped it.

"I'll be in San Marcos for a few days. I need you to be out of the house by the time I get back."

Doug doesn't object. Silence escorts me from the hotel room, and I feel so lonely I could die.

I encounter Ethan in the hallway by the elevators, crouching by the door.

"He's all yours," I tell him.

He jumps to his feet. "Vic, wait!"

I hand him the bottle of champagne I brought for Doug and me. "Some detective I am, huh?"

"Vicky, come on!"

"Don't let me ruin your night," I say and step into the elevator.

It's after midnight when I arrive at the hotel in San Marcos. My head is buzzing and I feel numb. The scariest thing is that I can't recall driving here. I know I was on the freeway—I had to be—but not much else has registered in my mind for the past hour.

I take the stairs and drag myself to the fourth floor. I quietly enter the room like a lifeless ghost. If I wake Anaya, I'll have to explain to her why I'm back early, and I'm not feeling up for it.

I set down my purse next to the TV and slip out of my shoes. As I tiptoe to the bed, I trip on a pair of shoes and fall on top of my roommate. She turns on the nightstand lamp and brightness spills onto her bed, illuminating the startled face of Agent Brestler pointing a gun at me.

"Are you freaking kidding me?" I blurt out, looking Anaya in the eye. "Has this whole world gone mad?"

I can't deal with this right now, so before my partners attempt to engage in a lengthy explanation as to why they are sleeping naked in the same bed, I grab my shoes and purse and storm out of the room, letting the door slam behind me. The sound echoes down the long, empty hallway and chases me into the elevator.

At the reception, I get myself another room. But before turning in for the night, I buy myself a bottle of rum and a six-pack of Coke at the small convenience store in the lobby. I can't even bear to look at the bed in the room. I climb into the bathtub instead, where I drink and cry and drink and laugh. There's no rational way to handle this night, so I decide to ignore it by drinking myself into oblivion.

25

It's ten o'clock in the morning when I step out of the hotel building and into the blinding sunlight. I light up a cigarette as I head to the parking lot. Anaya texted me two hours ago to meet her for breakfast in the hotel restaurant, but I was still out cold and missed it. I can't say I was too upset about it.

Brestler's car is gone, but Anaya's is still in the parking lot. She is leaning against the driver's door, covered by the shade of an olive tree. "Got my keys?"

I search for them in my purse then hurl them at her.

She catches the bundle of keys and hanging trinkets in the air then she opens the doors. "Since when do you smoke?"

"Since today. Got a problem with that?"

"What's with the attitude?"

"I guess you could say I had a rough night."

I open the door on the passenger side, put out my cigarette on the asphalt, and take my seat next to my partner.

Anaya fiddles with her keys. "Look, Brestler and I . . . It's nothing."

"None of my business," I say as I rummage in my purse for a piece of chewing gum.

"I understand, but I wanted to apologize for making you feel uncomfortable last night."

Hold yourself together, I warn myself. Please don't cry.

"Look, we are all adults here. Don't worry about it. How about we get some coffee and talk about our case?"

My request dangles in the air between us like an invisible barrier. It's quiet in the car. I can hear Anaya's nervous breathing.

I look at her to see what's causing the delay. She is watching me with her big brown eyes.

"Yeah, sure. Let's grab some coffee."

We pass two Starbucks buildings on our way, but Anaya is driving with a purpose. She eventually pulls into the drive-thru lane of a local coffee shop. The line of cars is long. I know I won't be able to escape the conversation. It's fine. I'm not mad at my friend. I'm angry with myself for being so blind and stupid.

"Where's Brestler?"

"He went in early to the control center. We'll meet him there."

"Any new developments since yesterday?"

"The fingerprint technician left a message on Brestler's phone this morning. He matched all the prints lifted from the condo to Meredith, her daughter, and the manager of the building. Not one unidentified print was found. His supervisor hasn't finished reviewing the results, but I won't get my hopes up."

"How about the jacket? Did they find any saliva on it?"

"I haven't heard anything back."

We order our coffees and drive to the San Marcos Police Department. The closer we get to our destination, the stronger my desire to see my mother is. I could sit around all day in an office, waiting for the results from the forensic lab or I could untangle the bundle of lies and secrets my family has laid out before me.

I vote for the latter.

I Google search for a rental car. Then I ask Anaya to drop me off at the nearby Enterprise office.

"Why do you need a car? You aren't still mad, are you?"

I sigh. "No. It's nothing to do with you and Brestler. Remember the phone interview between the Bureau and my parents you overheard?"

"Yeah."

"I need to get home and clarify a few things with my family."

"What about our investigation?"

"Unless a new lead turns up or a piece of trace evidence shows promise, there's not much I can do here right now. You and Brestler got this. You don't need me."

"Don't be like this, Vicky. Of course, we need you."

I pull the band from my hair and redo my bun. "That's not what I meant. I'll come back as soon as I can. I have to tie up some loose ends with my mother . . . in person."

"No problem, take my car. I can hitch a ride with Brestler."

I break into a peal of laughter. Anaya snaps her head toward me, eyeing me as if I've gone mad.

"Sorry, those words meant something entirely different to me yesterday, than today."

Anaya's full pink lips widen, and she joins in my laughter. "Oh, shit. I'm going straight to hell, aren't I?"

I touch her hand. "No, you're not. FBI agents are human too. Right?"

Our bout of laughter slowly dies down, and the serious air between us returns.

"What happened last night? Why did you come back early?"

At Anaya's question, a flood of memories washes away my upbeat mood, and I feel the long fingers of disappointment and sadness wrapping around my throat. "You wouldn't believe me if I told you."

Anaya shoots me a sharp look. "Try me."

As I stare at her, my eyes start twitching and begin to blur with tears. "I can't talk about it. Not right now."

We pull into a shady parking spot in front of the police department. "Did the bastard cheat on you?"

I don't reply; my gaze is unwavering.

"He did? Bloody hell! What a rotten-faced marabou stork! Narcissist peacock."

Anaya is livid. Her anger is intense. I suspect she lives by her own unique moral compass. She's upset about Doug cheating on me, yet she sleeps with Brestler—a married man with children.

"I can't do this right now. I need to get to Temecula." I blow my nose in a used tissue I find in my purse. "Are you sure you're okay with me taking your car? I should be back by the end of the day."

"Yeah, go. No worries." She hurriedly gathers her personal belongings and steps out of the vehicle. "I'll call you if we find something."

I search my purse for my phone. I'll need it for navigation. My fingers slip over a Ziploc bag and my altercation with Tyler at the Morongo Casino rushes back to me. I pull out the palm and fingerprints I lifted from my car secured in a plastic bag.

"Do you think you could drop this off with a fingerprint analyst? See if they can get a hit on these prints?" I hold out the package for my partner.

She takes the bag and inspects it in the sunlight. "Looks like an improv. You lifted it?"

I nod. "I used my eyeshadow."

"Do I need to know where it came from?"

"If we get a hit, I'll tell you. Could be something, could be nothing." I slip over the middle compartment and into the driver's seat. "And hey, could you put a rush on it?"

Anaya's face turns serious. "I'll see Brown about this. He probably has more pull around here than I do."

I close the door and turn over the engine, but before I drive off, I roll down the window. "If we keep this up, I'll owe you a huge debt I'll never be able to repay."

Anaya bends down and looks straight at me. "I don't keep tabs, do you?"

26

F our familiar cars are parked in the driveway of my
parents' home when I arrive at their house. Fred's
navy-blue Prius Prime is dwarfed by Heather's red
Ford 150, a permanent exhibition of the power struggle for
Dad's attention between the two of them. I pull in behind
my father's silver E-350 Mercedes glistening in the summer
sunlight. A family reunion is not what I expected, and it
takes two cigarettes to help me work up the courage to face
the music and go inside.

My mom knew I was coming home because I called
her from the road, so this feels like a setup.

I haven't talked to Fred in ages. I don't call him, and
he certainly doesn't lift up the phone to check on me. The
day I left home, our relationship was reduced to Christmas
cards and occasional Thanksgiving dinners. Fred is years
younger than me, but it wasn't the age difference that kept
us from growing deep sibling roots, it was our history
together. As the oldest child in the family, I was always
told to let things go, be the bigger person, make peace no
matter who wronged who, and Fred knew how to play the
game and get me into trouble. I was the child who had to
learn about responsibilities early in life, while Fred was

Mommy's boy. He never had to put in the hard work, yet enjoyed all the benefits.

We don't have a thing in common. We don't even look alike. Fred is nearly two heads taller than I am and has a hump on his upper back from hunching over his phone all day. His torso is like a barrel. His arms and legs are slim, but he doesn't have an ounce of muscle on him.

He was born before Susie was kidnapped, so he was spared the drama that followed that devastating night, though he suffered the consequences all the same. Mom never let him out of her sight nor allowed him to do anything where he might injure himself. Now he can't even change a lightbulb in his house, for which his wife, Sherrie, complains incessantly.

I'm closer to Heather; I always have been. Common interests bridged the five-year age difference between us. When we were younger and single, we used to go out together a few times a week to grab a drink, and we would call each other daily to report on our lives working in the men's world. We don't talk as much as we used to, but I follow her on Instagram.

Heather is a beautiful woman with a cascade of thick brunette hair and an intelligent look in her eyes. She works out regularly with her fellow firefighters at the station—an event she frequently shares on Instagram—and travels a lot with her boyfriend. They've been to Europe three or four times these past three years. She said my trips with Doug inspired her to see more of the world.

I suspect she isn't here today to tell me about her trip to Isla de Mujeres last month. So why is she here?

Somebody must have been spying on me from the window because I'm still in my car when the front door opens. Mom's ashen face comes into view. "Put that damned cigarette out and come inside!"

I flick it out the window, open the door, and step on it. "That's rich coming from your mouth."

"Seriously, Vicky, you don't have to follow all my bad examples."

I have a comeback for that, but I squelch it. I've already been too nasty to my mother, and I feel the emotional struggle inside of me. Making her the object of my frustration is wrong, and I know it.

"Come on, hurry up. The air conditioning is running!"

The new house has more space, a bigger yard, and was half the price of my childhood home, but I haven't warmed up to it yet. It feels cold to me, impersonal, and void of my childhood memories. There is no fresh pancake and maple-syrup smell mixed with the unmistakable fragrance of Bounce dryer sheets lingering in the air. No baskets of unfolded laundry perched at the end of the dining room table. No dirty shoes are scattered at the entrance. No yelling, music, and TV mixed into one continuous sound of madness. The house is quiet, organized, and reeks of lavender. The only connection I have to it is the overwhelming amount of framed family pictures on the walls. I feel more detached emotionally from this place than I ever have as I step inside the foyer.

I find my entire family seated in the living room. At the sight of me, my father switches off the TV and gets up from the recliner. My body turns into a log as he hugs me. I don't know this man. He might as well be the killer I'm chasing. He certainly travels to the same areas we've been investigating and had the opportunity to carry out the deeds without raising suspicion. A man who can hide his infidelity from the people he lives with can conceal anything.

He holds me at arm's length and looks me in the eye. "How are you, Vickybee?"

"Not as good as you, I suppose." I turn out of his clutch and face Heather and Fred curled up on the couch like when they were children. "It's not like I'm not happy to see you guys, but I thought Mom and I were having a private conversation today."

Mom steps out from the kitchen carrying a pitcher of lemonade and five cups on a tray. "The story your father and I will share with you today will affect all of you. We are a family. No matter what happens, we will always be a family. I want you to remember that, Victoria."

"Of course, you are my family. What are you talking about?"

"Please sit down, Victoria. Do you want a cup of lemonade?"

I lick my parched lips and take my place opposite the rest of my family, like the subject of an interrogation. I refuse the glass my mother is handing me, and she accepts my reaction without comment.

"You all know that I talked to the FBI yesterday, but you don't know what was discussed."

My father leans forward. "There is something we need to share with all of you."

"Let my mother finish!" I snap at him. He always takes the words out of her mouth, like he doesn't think she's capable of expressing herself without his help. His interruption irritates me now more than ever. "Dickie," I add to establish a mutual understanding.

The blood drains from my father's face as a blend of disbelief and shock punches him in the chest.

I don't care about being a disrespectful daughter. We wouldn't be in this mess if he hadn't have fathered bastards all over the country.

Heather is the first one to emerge from the silence. "What's going on, Mom? You're scaring me."

Fred removes his glasses and starts cleaning the lenses with the front of his shirt. "Did you guys do something illegal?"

My mother cups her face with both hands and leans forward. "Oh, Lord, please help me get through this day."

My ears began to ring, and I press my nails deep into my palms to channel my frustration. "Tell us what's going on! I can't take this suspense any longer."

Mom sips at her lemonade, then sets the glass down on the table with a clang. She kneels in front of me and takes my hands into hers. "I want you to know that I love you more than you can ever imagine. There is nothing I wouldn't do for you."

"Okay," I say, breathlessly, as an eerie feeling gnaws at my insides.

"You are my daughter, Victoria . . . but I didn't give birth to you."

My neck flexes. "What?"

"Your father and I took you in when you were born. You never met your birth mother."

"I'm . . . *adopted*?"

Mom is having difficulty looking me in the eyes. "I never wanted to tell you about this because I didn't want the truth to affect your life. You've grown into a beautiful and confident woman, and we are so proud of you. It doesn't matter how you came into this world or into our family. What matters is who you are now and who you choose to be."

"What are you talking about, Mom?" I hear Heather's voice, but it's faint in the background, as if my ears are refusing to hear more. "What do you mean Vicky is adopted?"

Mom stands up with the support of the coffee table, walks to the wall, and stops in front of a picture of me as a baby. "There was an . . . 'accident' at the care facility I worked at as a young nurse. We were caring for a young woman suffering from a serious spinal and brain injury following a car accident. She was unable to move, speak, or express herself in any way. Her name was Emma Alexis." She takes the picture from the wall and hugs it to her chest.

"She lost her parents in a motor vehicle accident. She only had her grandparents to look after her, but they couldn't provide her the medical care she required. They entrusted us with their granddaughter's care, and we looked after her for years."

My heart begins beating faster. I don't know where this story is going, but I have a bad feeling about it.

Mom hands me the picture. "Look at you, you were such a happy and beautiful baby."

"I don't want to look at the picture."

Tears stream from my mother's eyes. My dad hands her a tissue, and she blows her nose, sitting back down on the couch. "Something terrible happened to Emma. We were responsible because we were the ones who were supposed to protect her. But we didn't."

"Do you want me to continue?" my father asks, but I refuse to look at him.

"No, no. It's okay, honey. I want to tell Vicky what we did."

"Oh, Mother, what did you do?" Fred whimpers. I can't look at him either. I'm sitting alone, isolated, like a criminal, an outcast.

Mom takes another sip of her lemonade, then clears her throat. "The establishment was owned by a man named James Sullivan."

My suspicion curdles into fear.

"He was a kind man and a gentleman. Everybody loved him at the home—patients and employees alike. But he had a deadbeat brother, Angus. He was a loser. It was hard to imagine the two men were related. After three failed marriages and even more failed businesses, James took pity on his brother. He helped him start a window-washing and roof-cleaning business. James hired him for the care home, and he'd come by every couple of months with a crew to remove leaves and debris from the gutters, clean the glass panels that wrapped around the building, and power wash the tile roof. He also—" Mom looks at Dad in panic. "I can't say it, honey. I-I'm sorry. I can't."

Like a stone statue, I sit, unmoving. I want to encourage my mom to finish her story, but the words don't form in my mouth.

Heather sits down next to her and drapes her arm over her fragile back. "You can do it, Mom. Tell us what happened."

Every tragedy starts with a single event. Going down the road we shouldn't have taken, saying something we shouldn't have said, or doing something we shouldn't have done. Victoria Emma Collins was slowly dying inside. I was about to be reborn as someone else, I just didn't know who yet.

Mom takes a deep breath and holds it in, trying to buy time to find a better way to deliver the news she is about to bestow on us. On me.

She swallows hard and looks me in the eye. "Emma Alexis is your birth mother, Victoria. She is the one who brought you into this world."

"Wait! What?" I find myself sinking back into the couch so deeply, I'm nearly lost in its soft cushions. "I thought you said she was in a coma?"

"No, she wasn't in a coma; she was incapacitated. And Sullivan's waste-of-space brother took advantage of her. He raped her . . . only God knows how many times. And she got pregnant."

A jolt of shock, like a rocket, launches me to my feet, and I grasp my head because my brain feels like it will explode. "What are you saying?" I whimper. "That my real mother is a disabled woman and my father is, is . . . a *rapist*?"

Panic is coming. I crouch down before I faint.

"Here, drink this!" My father offers me a shot glass with a dark-mahogany liquid in it. "It's Jägermeister."

I drain the glass with one gulp. The burn is intense, but it can't overpower the throbbing pain in my head. The buzz comes fast—as soon as the liquor hits my empty stomach, and I falter . . . plop to the ground in shock. I feel Heather's body pressing against me.

"Where is she? My mother?" I whisper.

"She's passed away." I hear my mom saying. "Less than two years after you were born. Emma's grandfather had died, and her grandmother made the decision to remove Emma from life support."

I don't know those people. I have no memory or any connection to my real mother. Yet hearing about her death breaks my heart. I begin to cry like I've never allowed myself to cry before. All of my sorrow and grief about Susie's disappearance, my father's lies, Doug's betrayal, and now *this* come crashing down on me.

"It's okay. We'll get through this," Heather whispers into my ear, stroking my hair.

I'm so swallowed up in heartache and self-pity that I've almost forgotten the most obvious question—the one that's been dangling in front of my eyes for the last week.

"If I'm not your child. If I'm the daughter of a woman in a vegetative state. If I'm the result of a rape. Then who is Blake Sullivan? How can we be related?"

My mother opens her mouth, but the sound doesn't come out, and she looks like a fish gasping for air.

Dad puts his hand on her shoulder like a knight in shining armor coming to her rescue. "Blake Sullivan is your brother, Vicky," he says. "Your twin brother."

27

I'm disoriented and breathing slowly, my mouth emitting random wheezing sounds. I go to the kitchen, refill my shot glass with Jägermeister, and toss the drink down with one gulp. It flows down my throat like hot needles. I pour another one.

A hand gently presses against my back. I turn to look at my mother's pain-stricken face.

She removes a shot glass from the cabinet and pours herself a drink too. "I'm so sorry you had to find out about this under these circumstances."

My brain activity is all over the map, my mind firing out an array of thoughts and speculations.

"Blake Sullivan can't be my twin brother," I say with conviction. "His birthday is two months earlier than mine."

"There is an explanation for that. Blake *is* your twin. He was born a couple of minutes before you. The doctor who delivered you both managed the paperwork. He couldn't get birth certificates for the two of you dated the same day. We had to wait two months before we could register you."

"You were tampering with legal documents?" I'm on the verge of hyperventilating. My heart feels as if someone is stabbing my chest. "My birth certificate is fake? My god, what if they find out about this at the Bureau?"

"I didn't say anything about it to the FBI. I'm not that stupid."

I can't even look my mother in the eye. I grew up with a sense of pride, honesty, and integrity. She taught me all those things, but now my whole concept of what's right and wrong has been ripped out of me like a page from a book.

"I can't believe you were capable of coming up with this elaborate plan to deceive everyone."

"We had no choice. By the time we found out about Emma's pregnancy, an abortion would have been too risky, so we let her carry her babies to full term. James had an old doctor friend from college who helped with the delivery. Back in the 70s, that man was mixed up with a bad crowd. He eventually straightened out his life, but he still had connections from his old days. He was also the one who helped us illegally obtain birth certificates."

This whole conversation is visibly wearing down my mother. The black circles under her eyes have become darker, her eyelids deeply sagging, and her lips wrinkled and dry. I watch her closely, but I don't know what to say.

She pours me another glass of Jägermeister. "Nobody will ever know about your birth certificate. We never reported the crime. You were born in a nursing home, not a hospital. Your father and I claimed you as our own and took you home. My boss and his wife adopted the boy."

I let out a long, troubling breath. "I need a cigarette."

Mom opens the junk drawer and takes out a pack of Camel Blues. "Let's go to the laundry room. That's where I smoke when it's hot and humid outside, like today."

In our old house, the laundry room was a place for dirty shoes, sweaty jerseys, coolers, team flags, and a collection of single socks whose pair had mysteriously disappeared. The top of the dryer held an assortment of detergents and cleaning chemicals. A tablecloth draped over a shower curtain rod concealed the hardware on the wall behind the washer and dryer. Their new laundry room is quite the opposite: everything is clean and organized. Perfection.

I feel an urgent need to trash the place.

Mom turns on the exhaust fan and closes the door behind us. I light a cigarette for each of us.

"We did a terrible thing, Victoria. We covered up a heinous crime. But we needed to protect you and your brother."

"I didn't know you were such a scheming criminal mastermind. How come I always had to be the perfect kid growing up? You never cut me any slack. You would have skinned me alive if I cheated on a test at school!"

"What I did back then doesn't define who I am. And believe me when I say that it has haunted me every day since."

"Bad conscience, huh? I guess that explains your smoking and drinking."

My mom gives me a hard stare. "Don't be nasty, Victoria. It doesn't suit you."

I take a deep drag from my cigarette. "What happened to the rapist?" I can't bring myself to call that animal "father." Let alone digest the truth about my past. I don't consider my childhood a lie or a waste. My experiences growing up shaped me into who I am today. I won't allow myself to doubt who I am because my father was a rapist, a perverted criminal. Rapists aren't born. It's not a hereditary gene. It's not in my blood. But that man's blood runs in my veins. At the thought of it, a shudder runs through me, and I gag. I lean over the laundry room sink and upchuck the four shots of Jägermeister. I throw my burning cigarette into the slosh and wash it down with water.

Mom hands me a towel to wipe my mouth. She places the back of her hand against my forehead, checking for fever as if I were a little kid coming down with the flu. I jerk away. How can I ever trust her again if she is such an elaborate liar?

"I'll make you a cup of tea," Mom says, leaving the room.

"Wait!" I yell after her. "Where is he? Did you let him get away with it?"

"He's in prison."

Her answer isn't what I expected. "So, you reported him? Then how did you manage to pull off this scam?"

She takes a deep breath and blinks long. "It wasn't a scam, Victoria. We raised you as our own. We wanted you to have a happy childhood, a better life, not grow up in the foster-care system."

Blake didn't have a happy childhood. "How much time did he get for raping my mother?" I ask, cutting off her self-explanatory speech.

Mom's neck flexes, and she focuses her eyes on her hands. I now understand her frequent mood swings when I was a kid. One day she would be the funniest and cheeriest mom in the world, taking us to the movies or for ice cream. Then the next day she would fall into depression, having little to no patience with us.

"Twenty-five to life, with no possibility of parole for a minimum of fifteen years."

"Then he's out? He committed the crime more than thirty-four years ago. There's no way he'd still be incarcerated. When was the last time you checked on him?"

Mom leans her back against the doorframe, then slides down to the tile floor. I leap to her, grasping her arms. "Mom, are you okay?"

She touches my face. "I'm fine, just a little lightheaded. It all happened so long ago. It's difficult to talk about this. I've spent my entire life trying to make up for what we did, knowing that our secret would eventually come out. I always knew this day would come. The day when all the good deeds I've done throughout my life won't mean a thing and I'll be judged by the worst thing I've ever done."

I plop back onto my butt. "You didn't report him, did you? He's in prison for an unrelated charge, isn't he?"

My mom reaches for my hand, but I don't want her to touch me. I scoot away. I've looked up to this woman my entire life. I adored her and was ever-grateful for the sacrifices she made for me. But that person I loved isn't real. It was a role, a persona played by my mother and inspired by her guilt.

"I need you to understand why we did what we did."

"What reason could you possibly have for letting that animal get away with rape? Not to mention that if he was capable of assaulting a defenseless, incapacitated woman, what else was he capable of doing? I'm chasing a serial killer right now. For all I know, it could be him!"

She shakes her head. "I know what we did was wrong, Victoria. There are no excuses, but I was young, twenty-five years old when it happened. I wanted to report it, but James told me that if we went to the police, his business would lose all credibility. He told me that if his business went bankrupt, then everyone would lose their jobs. I worked with married couples, and families relying on the paycheck from the care facility. We thought that handling the situation in-house was the best option for everyone." As if a sweet memory came to her, Mom's face lights up with a shade of pink. "We painted Emma's room with colorful flowers and cute animals. It was beautiful. She loved it. She was never left alone again. There was music in her room, and someone was always with her, reading her books and showing her magazines. She was happy. We made her happy. That much, I do know."

The ball in my throat was growing larger, and tears pushed against my eyes. My chest rose and fell rapidly with my ragged breathing. That poor girl was my mother, my real mother. I'd never get to hug or kiss her, and she never had a chance to hug or kiss me.

"Why is the rapist behind bars now?"

"When we found out that he was the one who had been assaulting Emma, I wanted justice. We didn't report the crime, so my boss's brother was never charged for what he did, but I couldn't live with that. So, James cut a deal with his brother. He'd go to prison for grand theft auto, and in exchange, he would give up his children. Angus agreed. He spent almost two years in prison for stealing a significant amount of money from the nursing home, which, of course, never happened. When he got out, he wanted money and James paid him to disappear. After that, we didn't hear from him for years."

Mom blows her nose and continues. "When you and Blake were ten, James died in a terrible beach accident. Angus came back to town for the funeral and sought me out during the service. He said he wanted more money. I told him no. I tried to stay away from him, but he cornered me at the reception. He told me how cute you looked and how much you resembled Emma. He was a disgusting human being. He said the statute of limitation for rape is ten years in California, and he could no longer be prosecuted for the crime. He wanted his children back."

I feel my whole world collapsing around me. "Please don't tell me you paid that criminal."

Mom bobs her head. "We did. We had no choice. He was going to tell you who he was and threatened us that he'd go public."

"And you believed him?"

Mom wipes her nose. "We didn't want to let him hurt you. We loved you so much."

I lean forward and embrace the woman who raised me, who is my mother in nearly every sense of the word. As I hold her, she soaks my shoulder with warm tears and tightens her arms around me with all her might.

I kiss her head. "I love you too." I weep with her.

Heather opens the door on us. "Is everything okay?" She finds us cuddling on the ground and envelops us in her arms. "I'm sorry, Vicky. I'm so, *so* sorry!" she cries. "Dad told us everything. I love you so much. I even forgive you for spilling spaghetti sauce on that stupid shirt

I loved." It was the longest grudge Heather ever held against me when we were kids. "You are my sister, you'll always be my sister."

I push away from the group hug and wipe my face with my hands, then smooth back my hair and clamp it with a clip.

"Do you know where Blake is?" I ask my mother.

She shakes her head. "We tried to keep the two of you separated. We feared you to would develop a special twin-like relationship if you spent time together. In the long run, that would have made it harder on both of you. Then after James' death, I completely lost touch with the family."

"He was abused," I say, straight-faced. "After his dad, this James Sullivan died, his wife passed away too, and Blake was bounced from foster home to foster home. He was neglected. Pimped out. Used. How could you stand by and let that happen?"

Mom covers her face with her hand as if this is new to her. "I didn't know," she admits breathlessly. "I swear."

"How could you not know? You worked for Sullivan!"

"I did. But James sold his business a year after Emma was taken off life support. He couldn't face that place any longer. I left a year after James, when I was pregnant with you, Heather." She smiles at my sister. "We didn't keep in touch. It was too difficult to face each other."

"You should have looked out for Blake. Or at least checked on him after his parents died—I mean adopted parents." My chest tightens at the vivid images my imagination conjures up about Blake's suffering in childhood. I feel the darkness coming for me, and I want to hurt someone or something. Someone needs to pay for what they did to my brother. I feel a deep and intense hatred against the world. I want justice for him. I want him to know that I wasn't there for him before, but I'm here for him now. "You should have protected him."

"I understand how you feel, Victoria—"

"Do you? I don't think you do."

"I was young and naive. I thought I was doing the right thing."

"And where was Dad in all this?"

"He supported me fully."

I scoff. "Of course, he did. Deception comes easy for *him*."

Mom's eyes shrink. "What's that supposed to mean?"

"You guys want me to order a pizza or something?" Dad appears in the hallway, holding his phone.

"How can you think about food right now?" Heather reprimands him.

"No, Heather, he's right." I stand up and take a deep, cleansing breath. "I need to eat something before I pass out from low blood sugar. I haven't eaten anything today."

"I'll go and make that tea now, all right, sweetheart?"

"Sounds good, Mom. But before you go, you need to tell me where my . . . my . . . that man is incarcerated and why." I refuse to call that evil man "my father" and I never will.

"After he was released from prison . . . around 1988, he . . . he kidnapped and raped young girls. The police eventually caught him and prosecuted him."

"Fuck!" I blurt out, my last shred of faith in my mother dispersing into the air. "I hope you know that you and Sullivan are responsible for this."

My mom's lips quiver. "You think I *don't know* that?! Don't you think I blame myself and live with that *every freaking day*?!"

"Who'll tell that to the victims and their families?" I check the time on my phone. Three text messages from Anaya. I ignore them. "Where is he now?"

"Last time I heard, he was in a correctional facility in Banning, off the I-10 east of Riverside."

"I know the place," I say, astonished. "It's the same prison Blake did time."

28

My headache subsides after eating some of the
pizza my dad ordered, and my motivation to
find Blake switches into a higher gear. Since I've
learned about my brother's existence from my chief at the
FBI, it's been a roller-coaster of emotions for me, from
denial to shame to anger. At first, I wanted to find Blake to
clear my name and restore my integrity at work. But now
my sole focus is on bringing him into our family. He needs
to know he is not alone and has a family that cares. I can't
turn back time or right the wrongs he's suffered, but I sure
as hell can prevent history from repeating.

As I drive along the I-15 to the prison in Banning to
meet my biological father, my hands clench the steering
wheel hard. All I can think about is my brother being alone
in this world, having lost hope in humanity. His father is a
rapist. His mother was a helpless young woman who
passed away before her time. His adopted parents were
liars and cheaters. His aunt a trailer-trash crackhead who
neglected him. His foster parents pimped him out. The
system failed him. How can someone remain emotionally
stable and push forward in life with that kind of bleak
past? He might be living on the streets, doping to stay high

because that's the only thing that can help him to keep the dreadful thoughts and memories out of his head. Without a stable home environment that could have helped him to earn a higher level of education and without financial support from his family, I doubt he's crawled far out of the hole he's been pushed into his entire life.

My breathing becomes shallow as I consider Blake's life options. It could have easily been me in his shoes. Why wasn't it *me*? Who chose the two lives for us? Fate? God? Coincidence?

The ringing of my phone brings me back to the present. Anaya's calling. I answer the call knowing that I'm not in any condition to make excuses this time.

"Hey there, stranger, where are you?"

"I'm driving."

"Are you coming back?"

"Not yet." I keep my answers short to avoid lying.

"Do you need me to cover for you?" she sounds disappointed.

"If you don't mind. Just a little while longer."

"I hope everything's grand. You shouldn't be alone after last night. We all need help releasing pressure sometimes, or we'll implode."

"I'm not alone, but thanks for your concern." I sound way too formal, but I didn't expect her to bring up Doug. To be honest, I wasn't thinking about him or last night at all. The brain works in mysterious ways.

Anaya doesn't get the hint and keeps beating the dead horse. "I don't understand why Doug would risk losing you? For what, a one-night stand? Do you know the bird?"

It's not easy holding in several secrets. You can try to bury them or pretend they don't matter, but the dark secrets remain and spread like poison, rotting you from the inside. They are like cancer, growing and eating away the healthy parts of you. And like the chemotherapy that kills the healthy cells along with the cancerous ones, when you try to eradicate your toxic secrets, it will destroy another part of you as well.

"It wasn't some random *bird*. Doug cheated on me with a guy," I blurt out, feeling instantaneously relieved. The anonymity of a phone call has its advantages. A face-to-face confession would have been harder, even impossible for me.

A long silence ensues, then my partner's voice comes through weak and unsure. "Bloody hell! I don't know what to say. He cheated on you with a bloke?"

I don't know what I expect Anaya to say. What do you tell a friend who finds out her husband or boyfriend is playing for the other team? We live in a world where we are encouraged to do what we feel, be selfish, enjoy our lives as we see it fit, even if we hurt others, especially loved ones. Sacrifice and delayed gratification seem like ancient philosophies. So, even if I consider myself the victim here, I don't have the social acceptance to ask for sympathy.

I clear my throat. "You don't need to say anything."

"This is mental. Where are you going?"

"Don't worry I'm not going to do anything stupid to Doug."

"That's not why I was asking. But now that you brought it up. *Are* you going to do something stupid?"

I chuckle in desperation. "You don't need to worry about me. Doug is the least of my concerns right now."

"Okay. Tell me where you are? I'll meet you." I can hear the panic in Anaya's voice, and her concern for me is weakening me. It makes me soft. And now, when the truth is clawing its way out of my throat, I don't have the energy to push it back.

"I'm on my way to Banning to see my father at the Larry Smith Penitentiary."

Once again, my statement leaves my friend at a loss for words, so I continue. "My real father. The one who raped my mother thirty-five years ago."

"Fuck me! And here I thought that my relationships were a cock-up."

"Funny how a few weeks ago I thought my life was on the right track. Look at me now. My whole life went to shit."

Sirens echo through the dry, hot air stretching over the Interstate. I can't see the emergency lights, but I pull over to the side of the road.

"What's happening?!" Anaya screams into the phone. "Are you in danger?"

I spot the flashing red lights of a fire truck in my rearview mirror.

"Don't worry, they aren't coming for me. I'm not doing anything stupid. Right now, I'm on a mission to dig up the truth about my past. This morning I found out my mother is not my real mother and the man I've called 'Dad' my entire life is not my real dad. My birth mother was a young woman in a vegetative state, and my father was a fat-piece-of-shit loser who raped her at the long-term care facility she resided." My voice buckles at the end. I will never be comfortable talking about this.

"Oh, God, Vicky!" Anaya moans over the phone. "You found out about this all today?"

I suck my nose because I don't have a tissue. "I did. Great week I'm having, right?" I say, trying to joke my pain away.

Once the fire engine passes me, I pull back onto the road.

"You're going to see this man right now?"

"That's the plan. I want to look that disgusting pig in the eye and ask him how he could have done something so horrendous."

"Are you sure that's a good idea? Maybe you shouldn't go alone. How far are you from San Marcos? I could take Brestler's car and meet you there."

"I appreciate your offer, Anaya, but you have a serial killer to hunt. I promise I'll join you as soon as I can. But I need to find my brother first, my twin brother. It's how this whole thing began. A DNA analysis made the connection during my routine background check at the office. The chief suspended me because he thought I was purposely lying about having a brother with a criminal record."

"Bloody fucking hell! I need to sit down because I'm about to lose my shite. Jesus, Vicky."

"Oh, yeah, did I forget to mention that this co-called brother of mine is a criminal? He did some time for physically assaulting a woman, then he fell off the face of the earth about a decade ago, after he was released from prison." It feels awkwardly empowering and refreshing to talk to someone about my family's history. Somehow, I know everything will be okay because I'm no longer alone in this mess.

"The prints you gave me. Are they your brother's prints? That's why I'm calling. We ran them through in three different databases but didn't get a match."

"Geez, I nearly forgot. No, they aren't my brother's prints. Those prints were a possible lead I was following for our case." I don't know why I lie again. 'I guess I don't want to start another chapter of Victoria Collins's *A Series of Unfortunate Events* (In this story, not only is there no happy ending, there are very few happy things in the middle.)

"Maybe if we find a suspect, we'll be able to match the print to him, but until then, it won't be of any help."

The news hits me harder than I expected. I would have bet that Tyler had a criminal record. Aggressive and overpowering men like him usually don't stay off the police radar for long. I should have arrested him when I had the chance. My mother and Sullivan allowed my father to get away with a felony, and he used his second chance to rape more innocent women. If Tyler assaults someone, I'll be responsible.

Like mother, like daughter.

From my immature actions, shame descends on me. I rinse out the bitter taste in my mouth with some lukewarm water. I've never been so disappointed with myself.

I need to refocus my energy if I hope to untangle this mess. I need to let my friend go. "I gotta go, Anaya. I'll call you later, I promise."

"Call me if you need anything, love, all right?"

"Will do. And hey, if the chief calls about my absence, tell him I'm following up on a lead for our investigation. Would you do that for me?"

"I got you back, love. Don't you worry. Just don't do anything mental, alright."

"What do you consider mental?"

"Not funny, Vicky. I'll check in with you later. Make sure you answer your mobile! If not, I'll hunt you down. Understood?"

"Yes, ma'am." I smile. Anaya is getting really good at picking up my American English and mixing it with her native way of speaking. Though her accent will always give away her country of origin. And her love for tea and 'biscuits'.

I disconnect the call as I drive up to the security gate at the prison. It's a different guard this time, but the same protocol.

The deputy warden I met last time, who left the message about Gooden on my phone, is on duty today, but he's stepped out for a meeting with a supplier. His absence is to my advantage. I won't have to fabricate a story about needing to interview Angus Sullivan.

A guard escorts me to the same visiting room I met Paul Gooden a few days ago. I take a seat at a table in the farthest corner, facing the door. I want to take my time watching Sullivan shuffle through the room between tables and chairs, his hands and legs bound.

I spend my time waiting for him by skimming through his file. The man is eighty-six-years old. The fact that life allowed him to reach a ripe old age fills me with rage and what I read in his file just deepens my hatred for him.

According to the warden's notes, Sullivan is thriving in prison. The number of inmates under his command is estimated to be between fifty and sixty. He was suspected of being involved in dozens of attacks on prisoners and guards but was never convicted. A true hero I can be proud to call father.

An alarm blares and the door opens. My throat goes dry with fear, and my palms begin to sweat. It will take all my willpower not to drag this pig across the table and bash his head in for what he did to my birth mother.

A pale old man walks into the room. A limp in his left leg suggests an old injury. He looks well-fed and healthy but older than what I expected. Translucent, spotted skin stretches across his fat face. His thinning white hair is neatly combed back, like a freshly plowed field.

At the sight of the withered pathetic man, my anger slowly dissolves, and pity replaces my hate. I understand that him living this long isn't a blessing; it's a curse.

I watch him in disgust as he lowers himself onto a chair opposite me, the edge of the table wedged into the rolls of his stomach.

He places his folded hands on the table and looks me in the eyes through his smudged glasses, panting from exertion.

"What can I do for you, babyface?" he says in a harsh and wheezing voice.

I picture his liver-stained sausage fingers running up the thighs of my mother, his beard brushing against her breasts, and his breath fanning her neck. My teeth clench so hard it hurts.

"Angus Sullivan. The model citizen here at Smith's," I sneer through pursed lips.

"Call me Gus."

"Yeah, sure, whatever I can do to please you, *An*gus," I say, emphasizing his name.

His bushy white eyebrows lower and knit over his puffy red nose. He's irritated. Good.

I look for any resemblance between the two of us. I'm astonished to see that this monster has my eyes. Or rather, I have his. I feel my pulse quicken under the thin skin of my wrists. I put my hand on it to hide it.

Sullivan leans back in his chair and perches his hands on his belly. "You're Aimee's girl, aren't you?"

I'm unsure what shocks me more: that he knows who I am or that he didn't recognize me earlier.

"Where's Blake?" I get to the point. This isn't a social visit. I won't ask him why he did what he did to my mother. Nothing he could say would justify the brutal act he committed against Emma Alexis.

Sullivan lowers his chin. The wheezing sound he emits intensifies. "How should I know? If you haven't noticed, I'm a little confined in here. The real world is so far out of my reach, it doesn't even exist." He imitates a flock of birds with his fingers. His demonstration is rather childish.

"You must know something about him. You were both incarcerated here at the same time." I look at him for any sign of surprise at my statement, but he calmly looks on, telling me that he knew about Blake.

"Well, it seems he couldn't help but follow in his father's footsteps. Yeah, I met him. I taught him a thing or two."

"A thing or two about what?"

"How to survive in this nasty world."

I scoff. "The world is nasty because of people like you."

Sullivan smacks his lips. "Oh, yeah. Haven't you heard? Criminals aren't born, they groomed by life's other losers. Who do you think made me what I am?"

I smash my fist on the table, inadvertently attracting the guard's attention. "Millions of children grow up in abusive households, yet most of them don't turn out to be rapists and murderers. They chose to be good, to be better than what they saw at home. That's a lame and pathetic excuse your kind use to clear your conscience."

"You believe what you want to believe, babyface. It's easy for you to judge coming from a childhood full of unicorns and rainbows."

"Stop calling me babyface. I'm an FBI agent, not another vulnerable girl for you to manipulate."

"But you are my baby girl after all, aren't you? You found out the truth at last. That's why you're here, isn't it?"

My fingers roll into fists. I try to disperse my urge to repeatedly bash his self-assured face into the metal table.

"Does Blake know the truth? Did you tell him?"

"Of course, I told him! He's my son. He had the right to know."

I grasp my forehead and shake my head in disbelief. "Did you tell him about me?"

"Oh yeah! He was pissed off for a bit after learning you've lived a life of luxury while he was surviving on bread and water."

I swallow hard. "I didn't know . . . I would have helped him."

"Did the voices start talking to you in your head?"

"What voices?"

He leans close to me, and I can see every blemish and blackhead on his disgusting face. "The voice of regret. The voice of helplessness. The voice of failure."

I pierce him with my eyes. I won't let him play mind games with me. "You did this to us, you sick bastard. To Blake. You are to blame."

A hearty laugh erupts from him. "Whatever, babyface! All I did was have a little fun. The rest? Well, you can blame my brother and that sweet young nurse you call mommy."

I need air. I need to get away from this demon.

I jump out of my chair and rush to the door. "I'm done with this inmate!" I tell the guard.

I race out of the room, down the corridor, and out of the building. I lean over, holding myself up with one hand against the wall, trying to breathe. My head is dizzy, and I feel beside myself. If Blake knew about the Collins and me, why did he never contact us?

Once I manage to slow down my heart rate and compose myself, I call home. "Blake knows, Mom," I say, battling with my emotions. "Angus told him everything eight years ago."

29

I take a few minutes to emotionally recover from my first meeting with my biological father, the one I'll never call "Dad," before walking back to my car for a smoke. But after a short and intensive search under the car seats and in the glove box, I come up empty-handed. A sense of disappointment settles over me, and I bite into the skin on the inside of my mouth to punish myself for my forgetfulness.

I read Anaya's earlier texts to divert my attention from impulsively driving to the nearest gas station for a pack of cigarettes. That would be a new low, even for me.

I submitted the palm print you gave me. I'll call you when I hear back from the lab.

Old news. Delete.

Lyric called Brown. We watched the club's security footage. She identified two dozen guys who hung with Meredith. PDs on it. Nothing yet.

Sounds promising. Save.

Lab found saliva on Meredith's jacket. Enough DNA to analyze. Victory dance!

I should be happy about the new developments, but a hint of worry is slowly creeping into my gut. Even if we identify the man who spat on Meredith's jacket months ago at the bar, it doesn't mean he's the Piggyback Serial Killer and/or the serial rapist-turned-murderer the San Marcos sheriff is pursuing.

I put my phone away, wipe away the perspiration and dust from my face, and reapply mascara to make myself presentable. As Doug would've told me to do.

Doug—

For the first time since leaving San Marcos, I allow myself to think of him. Our whole relationship situation feels surreal. I don't think I've fully digested what's happened between us—what I have unveiled. And I don't think I ever will. Yet my image of him is shattered. My faith in our future is vaporized. But Doug's been a part of my life for so long and the thought of him no longer being around is daunting. I'm not looking forward to returning home to an empty house or to watch Doug pack up. There's nothing more depressing than watching someone you've loved carry his belongings out the front door and out of your life.

Going down this emotional lane makes me feel miserable. I can't afford to cry right now or feel sorry for myself. Mysteries are waiting to be solved.

I ruffle my hair and tuck my blouse back into my pants. I'm ready to return to the visitor center to meet Paul Gooden, Blake's former cellmate, for round two, when I spot a guard smoking by the side of the building. He looks to be my father's age—Collins, not Sullivan—but his bulging round belly, awkwardly combed sideways hair, and petite mustache may be adding years to his age.

I confidently walk up to him, introduce myself, and bum a cigarette off from him. He offers me an American Spirit with a sly smile.

The guard takes a deep drag from his cigarette. "No rest for the wicked, huh?"

"Unfortunately, criminals don't take weekends off." I inhale deeply from my cigarette and hold the smoke in my lungs until my head becomes dizzy, then exhale.

"I saw Gooden being brought up for you. He should be ready. If you don't mind me asking, why do you want to talk to that sleazebag? He's a good-for-nothing son of a bitch. Why is the FBI interested in him?"

"He was a roommate of the inmate I'm investigating." I put my cigarette out into the designated ashtray and offer the guard my hand to shake goodbye. As I lean in, I see his name on the tag pinned to his shirt. "Watson? I saw your name on a copy of a shift schedule from eight years ago. Do you remember a prisoner named Blake Sullivan?"

The guard's eyes shrink with suspicion. "Sullivan?"

"A twenty-four-year-old male inmate. Eight years ago, he finished eight months for breaking a woman's jaw? He was in Housing Unit 14?" I pull up Blake's mugshot on my phone and show it to the guard.

He plays with his mustache. Then, as if a lightbulb went off in his head, his eyes widen. "Oh, yeah! Blake Sullivan. I remember him. He's one of the few who hasn't returned. Most do."

"Yeah, he completely fell off the grid after being released from here."

The guard snaps his fingers at me. "You know what, I saw him leave. I remember asking him if he needed me to call a taxi or someone to pick him up. He walked to the bus station over there and left without a word." He points toward a narrow road shooting out of the complex.

I can't believe my luck. "Did Sullivan leave any contact information you know about? Or say where he was going?"

The guard's brows knit in deep concentration. "No, I don't think so. I remember finding it strange that he took the bus because there was a gal who wrote him letters all the time. I can't recall her name, but I remember Sullivan telling me about her. She responded to an ad—I think— Sullivan put in the classified section of a Christian newspaper. Or it may have been a chat room where they met. Anyways, he showed me a photo. She was a pretty young thing."

"Do you remember her name?"

Watson purses his lips, then clicks his tongue. "Nope. Sorry. It's been a while."

As quick as my erupting optimism arrives, it evaporates. Without a name or face, it would be downright impossible to find Blakes's pen pal.

I pull out my notebook and the Morongo Casino pen from my bag. "Could you describe the woman to me as best as you can? Hair color. Eye color. Any distinct features?"

Watson chuckles at my notepad. "Old school, I love it. Most cops record stuff on their smartphones nowadays."

I lift the pen in my hand and smile. "I'm not a fan of electronics. Too many little connecting parts to break. Back in college, a virus wiped out six months of work on my computer. Now when I conduct an investigation, I stick with this trusty notebook. Plus, victims don't want to hear about technical problems affecting the chances of a perp being caught and punished. It happens more than you'd think."

Watson watches me silently; his gaze reflecting warmth. We've connected. I smile at him.

He points a crooked finger at my paper, indicating for me to start writing. "The chick was young, or at least in the picture I saw of the girl—twenty perhaps. Her hair was purple or pink, I don't remember exactly, but I remember warning Blake about her. She looked like trouble. She wasn't your typical Christian girl."

"Do you remember anything else about her? Name? Height? Where she lived?"

At my bombardment of questions, all I get from the guard is a series of grimaces and headshakes. "Her face was pretty. Lots of makeup though."

"Any moles? Tattoos?"

He shrugs his shoulders, offering me another cigarette. I politely refuse. "Come on, missus, it was almost ten years ago."

I flip the cover closed on my notebook, understanding this interview is finished.

"You've been a big help. Thank you, Officer. I'd better get inside. Gooden must be getting restless waiting for me."

"Let him wait. He has nothing but time." Watson is persistently holding out the pack of American Spirits.

I stay and have another smoke with my new favorite person on earth. He complains about the union and all the new regulations hampering the guards but giving more freedom to the prisoners. I don't comment. I represent the Bureau and refrain from sharing my personal opinion.

When our cigarettes burn down, I thank Watson for his help and pat him on the shoulder before heading to the main door.

"Jenna!" I hear him yell after me. I turn. "Her name was Jenna. Never got her last name but I'm pretty certain she was called Jenna."

Armed with a sense of victory bestowed upon me by this vital new information, I enter the visitor's room to meet Paul Gooden. Bursting with newfound confidence, I expect myself to dominate our conversation. At the sound of the opening door, the prisoner lifts his head and starts rubbing his bald cranium with both hands, smiling teasingly.

"Agent Collins, it's good to see you again."

I pass the officer guarding the wall and stand by the table where Gooden is seated. "Let's skip the pleasantries and proceed to the meat and potatoes of why I'm here."

Gooden leans back in his chair; his face crestfallen. "Come on, Agent Collins. I'm locked up with a bunch of dudes in here. You won't deny me a little chitchat now, will ya?"

My need to pursue the new piece of information I've acquired is making me restless, and this silly teasing game between us is irritating me even more than the last time we met.

"Look, Paul, maybe wasting the time of an FBI special agent is exciting for you, or maybe you're looking for a story to share with your fellow inmates, but I already have the information I need. So unless you spit out what you know about Blake Sullivan, I'm out of here." I smack my hands down on the backrest of the empty chair in front of me, refusing to sit down.

"So . . . what's her name?" Gooden teases.

"Not like it's any of your business, but to prove to you I'm not bluffing, it's Jenna. Her name is Jenna."

I grin and wink at the handsome inmate, then turn to start heading for the door.

"You know where she lives?" Gooden shouts after me.

Shit! I'm the baited fish again.

I take a deep breath and turn to face the guard. I pull out a twenty-dollar bill from my pocket and hand it to him. Would you mind sending someone down to the commissary to bring Mr. Gooden—" I look at the inmate to finish the order for me.

"Two cheeseburgers, a large Coke—Coca-Cola, not that Pepsi shit—two cinnamon rolls, and a bag of gummy worms."

Annoyance registers on the guard's face, but I nod at him solemnly. He takes the money and leaves the room.

I return to the table and sit down facing Gooden. As he smiles, the teardrop tattoo under his eye stretches into a bell shape.

"Jenna Davis was her name. She lived with her husband in Lake Elsinore but spent most of her time at her parents' farm in Moreno Valley. I guess her husband worked a lot and she didn't like to be alone."

I don't show my informant how fired up I am about this new lead and manage to remain calm, even though I'm about to jump out of my skin. This is the first usable information I've been given about my brother since I started searching for him.

I casually flick open the cover of my notepad. "Do you have an address for this Jenna?"

"You really want me to do all the work, Vicky? Then why do the taxpayers pay you?"

"Don't push your luck, *Paul*." I can be personal too.

As we wait for the food, Gooden complains about the prison food and his accommodation, masterfully holding back the information he expects to be paid for first. I listen to him impatiently.

The door creaks open behind me, and a young guard enters the room with a tray bearing my order at last. I take the tray from him and set it on the table. Gooden reaches for a burger.

I put my arm across the food. "Nope. Not yet. You said Jenna had a husband?"

Gooden gives me a dark look and folds his arms, but the mouthwatering scent of the cheeseburger is too strong to resist. He takes a deep breath, then assumes a friendly posture. "Blakes insisted that his girl was done with that fool. Blake was her way out of his marriage."

"A convicted felon was her way out of her marriage? How bad could her husband be?"

The inmate shrugs.

"Have you heard from Blake since he was released?"

He shakes his head, eyeing the array of delicacies.

"Do you have an address or not?"

"I don't, alright? Try checking the logs from the visitor's desk. It'll have visitor names, addresses, and whatnot."

I ease the dish toward Gooden, thanking him for his help. As he's stuffing his face with the first burger, he blabbers that he'll be released in nineteen months, in case I want to meet up. I touch his hand appreciatively and steal a few gummy worms from the bag, holding his stare. It's better to part on good terms. I may need him again.

When I'm at the door, Gooden calls out to me. "Would you do me a favor, Vicky? Tell the lovely Mr. Zielinski that I did what he asked. I was a good boy, so he owes me a biscuit."

I give him a thumbs up and leave the room.

30

Doug's Instagram feed shows no signs of his distress. On the second day of the realtor convention, he's giving speeches and meeting people, commemorating every moment with pictures and short videos as if last night never happened. It's business as usual for Doug. His new way of recording himself, talking while driving, makes him look borderline arrogant and reckless. The motivation behind it eludes me. Are we supposed to believe that he doesn't have a minute to spare in his busy life to sit down and talk into a camera? Yet, his videos receive thousands of views. People hang on his words of wisdom like grapes on a vine.

The comments are pouring in for his *posed* action shots.

You are an inspiration, Doug! Keep it up!

Love your attitude! XXOO

Sexy! A heart and fire emojis.

You look amazing! #rockstar

I close the app and pay the cashier at the gas station for the case of White Claw Hard Seltzer and pack of Marlboro Lights I'm planning to attack this evening. But first, I need to meet Barbara Sullivan in Beaumont. I'm not thrilled to see the woman who allowed those horrible things to happen to my brother when he was young, but she is a lead I must pursue.

I don't get far down the road. I end up pulling into an abandoned parking lot, where I pop open a can of raspberry-flavored White Claw and light a cigarette. I recline my seat and set my head against the headrest. I picture myself in bed, sleeping peacefully, while Doug is on his laptop, drooling over photos of sexy men. I imagine him making love to me while closing his eyes and pretending he's touching Ethan's naked body instead. The hurt is finally catching up to me, and I feel a twisting pain in my stomach. Shedding a few tears would help release some emotional stress, but FBI agents don't cry. Do they? So I suffer in silence for a while.

When I finish my drink, I put out my cigarette. I hide the empty can underneath my seat and pull back onto the road. I listen to Teen Pop radio on Pandora to cheer myself up, but the silly and naive lyrics aren't helping me cope.

Soon after entering Beaumont, I pull up to Barbara Sullivan's house and park in front of a temporary chain-link fence. The house is under construction. The windows are taped off, and the roof and sidewalks are covered with plastic sheets. A crew of men in white coveralls is painting the exterior walls. The front door is open. I can see the inside of the house has been gutted. A truck's warning signal is beeping as it backs up into the front yard. A faded sign on a cargo truck advertises Miguel's Cabinets. It appears trafficking children and dealing drugs pays well if Blake's deadbeat aunt can afford such an extensive renovation on her house.

I holster my handgun, hide my laptop underneath the floormat in the back seat, and get out of the car.

"Excuse me!" I call out to a massively overweight man huffing and puffing his way to greet the truck driver. He stops to look at me, or at least I think he does—his dark, oversized sunglasses conceal his eyes.

"Yeah?" he says, wiping the sweat from his brow with a handkerchief.

After identifying myself, I ask for Barbara Sullivan. The man informs me that the bank foreclosed on the house and the woman who used to live here has moved to the Paradise Homes trailer park. He is quick to tell me that he barely knows the lady. He purchased the home at an auction a year ago for his family, but the house was vandalized shortly after that. The insurance company finally paid him for the damages. He rants about being cheated out of his fair share and holds a piece of paper with the address to the trailer park hostage until he finishes his irrelevant story.

A few minutes later, I'm on the road again, covered in dust and sticky with sweat.

The name, Paradise Homes, insinuates a wealthy gated community with swaying palm trees, artificial lakes, and a golf course. It may have been the case fifty years ago, but now the place is ugly and neglected. The shack for the security guard is vacant. It appears it has been that way for some time.

I drive slowly, making my way along the cracked asphalt road radiating hellish heat. I pass dilapidated mobile homes overgrown with dry wildflowers. A few updated houses remain and seem to be standing strong against the wave of poverty enveloping the area and the unforgiving power of the sun.

As I turn down the first street branching off the main road, I spot a person in a wheelchair. I pull over to inquire about Barbara Sullivan's residence. The man has no idea who I am talking about.

I keep driving.

At the next street, I find an elderly couple sitting on their porch. Three Pomeranians begin barking over each other as I approach them. They don't know anybody in the community by that name.

On my fifth attempt, I come across a young transient-looking man suspiciously dressed in a hoodie and jeans despite the roasting summer heat. He pulls his hand out of his pocket and points to a faded pink mobile home about a block down the road.

The tiny home stands alone at the end of the street. Overgrown with scraggly unpruned trees and shrubs and in desperate need of repair, like a giant toy car left in a field. I sigh in relief, grateful that Blake didn't have to grow up here.

I saunter through an open gate, hanging broken on its hinges, reading inspirational quotes painted on wooden signs covering the side of the trailer.

"The art of knowing is knowing what to ignore."
Rumi
"Breathe in the good shit. Breathe out the bullshit."
Unknown

"Sometimes people forget their own
greatness."
Jason Mraz
"A word to the wise isn't necessary — it's
the stupid ones that need the advice."
Bill Cosby

And several others about drinking wine.

I gently knock on the door, worried that the slightest force may break it. A dog is barking in the distance and a shrieking hawk swoops high above me across the pale-blue sky.

"Who is it?" a grumpy old voice seeps through the cracks.

I lean in, moving my mouth closer to the gap. "Hello. I'm Vicky Collins from the FBI. I'm looking for a Ms. Barbara Sullivan."

Silence. The dog's yelping rages on in the background.

I rap on the door again. "Hello? Ms. Sullivan?"

"What do you want? I wasn't expecting any visitors. I'm not decent."

I count to three to prevent myself from breaking down the door. "I would like to talk to you. It will only take a few minutes of your time," I say with patience, then improvise. "We can do it here, or I can take you down to the station. Your choice."

"On what charges?"

"Why don't you open the door and make this easier for both of us?"

A squeaking sound. A loud thud. A crashing and breaking sound as if someone was knocking stuff over in the house.

"Come in."

I push the door open. A burst of stale, putrid, warm air rushes at me from the inside. In the dim light, I spot a woman sitting in a wheelchair, pulling an oxygen tank as she approaches me.

She coughs, clears her throat, and spits into a tissue. I flip on a light switch to my right.

A soft, weak glow spills onto a poorly furnished room and a skeleton-like elderly woman in her nightgown.

"Turn it off!" she screams at me. "You think electricity grows on trees?"

I do as she asks, then I leave the door ajar to allow light into the small home.

I expected to find a monster within these walls—a vicious, heartless woman. But all I see before me is an old, withered person suffering from terrible health. I try to hold onto my anger and hatred, but it's slipping away.

I don't want to let the feeling go. This woman is responsible for my brother's childhood sufferings. She needs to pay for neglecting him.

"Are you Barbara Sullivan? Sister to James Sullivan?"

The woman adjusts the oxygen tube in her nostrils. "Obviously. Why do you want to know?"

"You the designated legal trustee of James Sullivan's estate after his death, including guardianship over his son, Blake, correct?"

The woman's face drains of blood, and her saggy eyelids rise. "That's old news. I don't have any money left if that's what you're after. You can tell that little shit that he won't get a dime from me. I raised his sorry ass. Wasn't that enough?"

My fingers roll into balls, and I hide them in my pockets before I punch the table.

"I'm not here for any money. I'm looking for Blake Sullivan."

She rolls herself to the table, dragging her oxygen tank along, where she pulls out a joint from a Ziploc bag and lights it. "It's medicinal. I have a prescription. Lung cancer, you see."

I wasn't raised to wish ill on anyone, but hearing that bit of information makes my heart jump with joy.

"But I don't, so how about putting it out while I'm here. Thank you," I say this more as an order than a request.

She ignores me and inhales deeply before exhaling right at me. "Why are you asking me about Blake? He never visits. I need help, you know? Someone to get my medications and bring me groceries. That little shit never stops by to see if I need anything. After everything I did for him, I would appreciate some gratitude." She points her thin crooked finger at me. "There's no justice in the world."

Seeing her suffering in pain, penniless and broken, I think that yes, there is justice in the world.

I step beside her, pull the joint from between her fingers, and drop it into a glass half full of black water and cigarette butts on the coffee table. "When was the last time you had contact with your nephew?"

"Hey! What did you do that for? You need to reimburse me for that joint! Good green ain't cheap."

I wipe my hand in a tissue. "File a complaint with the Bureau."

She lifts a cup of something that smells like cheap acidy wine from the table and drinks from it. "What do you want from me? Why are you harassing me?"

"Just answer the question, ma'am, unless you want to spend a night in lockup."

"This is police brutality. I want a lawyer."

"I'm FBI. I'm not the police."

She nervously pulls up the bottom of her nightgown, exposing her blotchy skin. She rubs her calves then gets out of the wheelchair, holding the oxygen tank for support.

"Like I said, I haven't seen the boy in years. He came by the old house a few years back, dressed elegantly, gloating like he was somebody. I asked him for money, but he laughed in my face. That's why I never wanted kids. Children are ungrateful little bastards."

"Did he say where he was living or leave a phone number? An address? Anything?"

The old hag tilts her head to the side, grinning like a madwoman. "You guys can't find him, can you? What did he do this time? Why am I not surprised?" she chuckles. "You'll never find him, you know? That boy might be full of himself, all selfish and whatnot, but he's smart. If he doesn't want to be found, well, you won't find him. I can assure you that. The kid has street smarts you can't begin to figure out."

"Is that a no?" I can't have another dead end.

"He has properties all over. He had a house in Lake Elsinore, one in San Diego, a condo in Corona. He came here to rub his wealth in my face; all suited up like some fancy businessman. I told him he owed me. I taught him how to survive in this world. I made him strong. And how does he repay me? He spits in my face."

"I read the social service's reports. You did Blake no favors. You took his inheritance and spent it. You put that poor little boy through hell growing up."

"Bullshit!" she blurts out, grasping the tank with both hands. "Show me proof! That corrupt little bastard is a pathological liar."

My nails are digging into my palm, rage is bubbling within me. I think of my Glock tucked underneath my jacket. I should put a bullet between this wicked woman's eyes and rid the world of her wormy existence. But calling her a worm isn't fair. Earthworms are essential to the planet, they have a purpose.

"Now be a good gal and refill my glass. As you can see, I have difficulty moving around." She extends her hand toward me with the empty cup in it.

"How about you give me an address to one of Blake's properties, and I'll do as you ask."

She eyes me suspiciously. "What did you say your name was? I didn't see you showing me any identification. You know what, I think I'm gonna call the police now." She starts shuffling toward the white phone covered with dirty fingerprints hanging on the wall.

"Really? Who do you think the cops will believe? An FBI agent or a burned-out, doped-up alcoholic?" I step in to block her path. "Now go fetch me those addresses before I push you down the stairs in your wheelchair and leave you for dead."

A mixture of panic and fear registers on her face. "Who are you?" she says through trembling lips.

"If I were you, I'd worry about getting me the information I asked for. Now!"

She points to the kitchen. "There's a drawer in there, on the left, underneath the toaster."

I follow her direction to a kitchen cabinet. "This one?"

"Yes, that's the one. Pull it out. You'll find a bunch of yellow post-it notes in there. Blake never gave me any addresses, but I overheard him talking on the phone when he visited me that one time. He was talking to a handyman about fixing a leaky roof. The address Blake gave the guy is written down on one of those post-it notes."

I rummage through a collection of batteries, pens, lip balm, and pennies. I finally find the address. "This is it? Lake Elsinore?"

"Yes, that's the one. Now leave me alone."

"Do you have his San Diego address?"

She shakes her head.

I slip the note into my pocket.

"So, where's my drink?" she groans.

I step in front of her and shove the empty glass into her hands. "Why don't you get it for yourself?"

I rip the door open and hurry out of the dingy home to be greeted by a dark and angry sky. The wind is blowing in strong gusts, nearly pushing me off the patio. What the hell happened to the weather?

A massive bolt of lightning strikes against the gray clouds overhead, followed by a loud clap of rumbling thunder.

A flash-flood warning alert dings on my cellphone. It's been a crazy summer in southern California. Heavy rains and floods one day, then a hundred degrees Fahrenheit heat and raging wildfires the next.

I pull my jacket tight around me and dash back to my car. Protected from the elements, I take out the note from my pocket. The address strikes me as being vaguely familiar. I pull out a case file from my bag and compare the address to the visitor's log from the penitentiary.

It's the same address as Jenna Davis's.

My heart begins hammering inside my ribcage. Blake is so close I can hardly believe it.

I slide the key into the ignition, light a cigarette, and crack the window. My heart is leaping out of my chest from a combination of excitement and nervousness. In an hour, after thirty-four years, I may finally meet my twin brother and bring him back to the family.

Then my conscience gets the better of me. I look back at the house and the front door I left open. I click my tongue and roll my eyes, as I turn off the car. Then I return to the home where I refill the old hag's glass with wine and make her a quick sandwich, all the while clenching my teeth. I feel conflicted about helping out Blake's self-absorbed, uncaring aunt, but I don't have to be the bringer of justice. Fate has already punished this woman.

My mother would be proud of me.

31

I feel conflicted about how to best approach my brother for our first encounter. Considering his criminal past, he likely has zero trust in authority, so going to his house as an FBI agent might scare him away. I could begin by introducing myself as his long-lost twin sister, but judging by Blake's lack of interest in finding his real family, even after our biological father told him about us, suggests he wants nothing to do with me.

The confusion swirling inside of me is making me nervous and insecure. I open another can of hard seltzer, and the moment I swallow the last drop, I know it was a bad idea. I lean onto the steering wheel, lightheaded and queasy. I need some solid food in my stomach to soak up the alcohol.

I search the internet for nearby fast-food restaurants to grab a quick bite. It doesn't take long to find out that my options are limited to a few spots. My stomach is too sensitive for a greasy burger or a spicy taco, so I opt for a salad at El Pollo Loco.

The Mexican fast-food restaurant is in the opposite direction from where I'm going, but I don't mind the delay. To be honest, I'm trembling with fear at the thought of meeting my twin brother for the first time and at the prospect of facing our terrible past together.

Our birth mother was a young woman in a vegetative state. She lost her parents in a car crash as a child and has since passed away. Our father, still alive and in prison, is a low IQ sexual deviant and vicious predator who took advantage of young women. It's no longer a secret that Blake and I are the results of an unimaginable rape; that we were ripped from our mother's arms and from each other at birth. And although I had a happy and safe childhood, surrounded by people who loved me, my brother was forced down the path of suffering and humiliation.

I expect Blake to resent me, but that doesn't mean I'm not eager to meet him and attempt to build a relationship between us. I'm anxious to get started, but some extra time to gather myself won't hurt.

As I drive to get food, I tell myself to be realistic about my meeting with Blake. As an FBI agent, I'm aware that the success rate for rehabilitating criminals is low, as most are simply too broken to mend. Yet as a sister, I want to believe that with love and care, I might be able to help heal my brother's heart. Time will tell which option comes true. But I know I won't give up on my brother, like so many others have in his life.

I order a chicken salad with extra avocados at the drive-thru window of El Pollo Loco, then park in the shade to consume my dinner.

As I eat out of the plastic bowl on my lap, I text Anaya: Just checking in. Everything is good here. Found some new information about my brother. Got his address. About to visit him.

A second after I hit send, my phone rings.

"I'm sorry for not calling earlier. It's been crazy here," Anaya pleads. Low-volume music and the sound of traffic are in the background. She's driving.

"No worries. I wanted to let you know that I'm still on the case and making progress."

"That's great to hear! I wish I were there with you to support you through all of this, but we finally have a solid lead, and I can't leave right now."

A pang of jealousy hits me. "What kind of lead?"

"Oh, I meant to text you. Things are moving fast. We received the DNA results back from the lab and got a hit on the saliva sample from Meredith's jacket. The perp is a convicted felon with some misdemeanors. His name is Sullivan. Blake Sullivan."

The shock literally jerks my entire body back in the car seat. My fingers cramp, grasping the phone tightly, as my whole body tenses up. "S-say that name again?"

"Blake Sullivan. Born September 29, 1985, making him thirty-four years old. Right now, we only have an old mug shot, but we're working on getting something more current. The search of Meredith's apartment turned up a receipt from May 10, from a place called the Stag Bar in Newport Beach. The date coincides with Portia's and the parents' statement. We've already asked Meredith's friends to verify the name of the bar as the place where the alteration took place. Lyric said she wasn't there when it happened, but she'd often go to the Stag Bar with Meredith and some other girls to hook up with rich guys, insisting the men weren't sugar daddies, that they were looking for, quote, "true love" at the popular beach town bar. The place is about a twenty-minute drive from San Marcos. Brown and I are heading there right now to review the security videos. I'll text you the mugshot of Sullivan to keep you in the loop."

The fork falls from my hand and lands in the salad. "No need to send me the picture, Anaya. I know what Blake Sullivan looks like. I mean, I know what he looked like eight years ago."

"What? How? Did Brestler already fill you in?"

"No . . . It's . . . I'm searching for Blake Sullivan myself: he's my twin brother."

"What?! Are you serious? That was . . . unexpected. You can't . . . I-I had no idea," Anaya stutters, struggling to find the right words.

"It's his spit on a jacket, right? It doesn't necessarily mean that Blake is the Piggyback Serial Killer."

"No, it doesn't, but you're on the team, Vicky. You read the behavioral profile on the serial killer. You were the one who discovered the patterns. Sullivan fits the bill."

"You don't know that with certainty. My brother disappeared nearly a decade ago! Nobody's heard or seen him since then. Not a parking ticket. No rental contracts. No home purchases. Nothing. He never even renewed his driver's license. For all we know, he's dead."

A long pause. I listen to my racing heart filling the silence.

Anaya speaks first. "You said you had a lead on your brother; what did you mean by that?"

I ponder my partner's question for a moment. Withholding information from the FBI could easily lead to termination of my employment, or worse, a felony charge. But by giving up my brother, I'd be subjecting him to endless scrutiny and investigations. I believe in our system, but it's far from perfect. Many people have suffered and will continue to suffer from injustice. I couldn't bear being responsible for my brother being dragged through the mud for something he may not have done, especially after what the system has already put him through.

"Uhm, yeah, . . . I have an address in Lake Elsinore, but my source isn't exactly reliable. I'm not sure if it's usable intel, so I'm heading there now to see if it checks out."

"I don't think that's a good idea, Vicky. Not only because he could be your long-lost brother, which makes him family and per protocol, you should be off the investigation, but because he may be a brutal serial killer. Your life may be in danger. I need you to stand down and wait for Brestler and me . . . I need you to text me the address."

Anaya's cold and authoritative demeanor slices through me. Then I remember that Detective Brown from the San Diego Sherriff's office is with her in the car, which would explain her hostile behavior toward me. I calm myself down, but I can't help feeling protective of my brother.

"Come on, Anaya! We found Blake's DNA on a jacket from a bar quarrel that happened months ago. It doesn't prove he's our killer."

"Yesterday, you were convinced that the two events were connected. You asked me to put a rush on the DNA analysis. Didn't you? That's why I'm now ordering you to stand down. I understand your position, and before we jump to any conclusion, I'll get the video footage from the bar. We'll be able to verify if Blake Sullivan was the one who attacked Meredith, then I'll head up to Lake Elsinore. Don't forget to text me the address. Understood?"

"Will do. Thank you, Anaya. I'll see you in a few hours."

"Vicky!" she calls out to me, and I hold the phone away from my ear for a moment before bringing myself to listen to her warning, which I know is coming. "Do not, I repeat, *do not* contact or engage Sullivan without me, am I clear?" We are no longer friends. She is my superior officer. She is my boss and the one who gives the orders.

"Understood," I agree, placing the salad bowl on the floor by the passenger seat and starting the car.

There is no way I'm going to let the police or FBI swoop down on my brother without concrete proof that he had something to do with Meredith's murder. I want to catch the killer as much as the next guy, but my brother has already suffered enough. I won't let him be made the scapegoat for the Bureau so it can look good in front of the media.

I enter Blake's address into Zillow to gather information about the property. It's a three-bedroom, two-bath, 1,100-square-foot house on a secluded half-acre lot. The house has been up for sale for over three months. The last registered sale was in 2007, which gives me hope. Barbara Sullivan overheard Blake reciting the address on the phone three years ago. Since then, there hasn't been a change in ownership. He should still be living there with his girlfriend, Jenna Davis.

I sweep through pictures of the property on Zillow. The rooms are done up in a Safari style décor of brown and moss-green color schemes. The curtains and upholstery parades in zebra and wildcat patterns. Each space is busy with useless collectible items and clutter. I zoom in on the pictures hanging on the wall, but they only contain manufactured shots of African mammals.

Slightly disappointed about not seeing a picture of Blake or members of his family in the photos, I switch off my cellphone and hit the road. I promised Anaya I wouldn't make contact with Blake before she arrives with Brestler, but that doesn't mean I can't scout the place before they get there.

Fueled with nail-biting anticipation and emotional terror, I merge onto the freeway, navigating the ever-increasing traffic on Saturday night. Twenty minutes out from the house, a mass of cars is stopped dead in front of me on Highway 74. Cussing colorfully, I roll down the window and light a cigarette. I remember many summers ago scarcely any cars used these roads. Now it's deadlock or near-deadlock traffic all day long.

Twenty minutes and three cigarettes later, I haven't traveled more than a mile. There must be a bad accident up ahead. I turn on the radio to find a station with local traffic information. Spanish music. Commercial. Christian preaching. Commercial. Rap music. Classical radio. Religious doctrine. Spanish music. Commercial. Crap! Now I remember why I stopped listening to local radio stations.

I switch off the radio and search my phone for traffic updates. Google navigation shows gridlock from here to Lake Elsinore and beyond. What the hell is going on?

I read a few breaking news articles online about the area. According to Newsweeks.com and Patch.com, a lightning bolt struck the parched hillsides below the Ortega highway starting a small fire, and due to strong winds, the wildfire is rapidly spreading through the canyons and racing toward residential homes. An evacuation order is in effect for the area. I search the map. The fire is threatening the community where Blake's house is located. I smash my fist onto the dashboard, scowling and muttering obscenities underneath my breath. Hell has fallen upon paradise, yet again, and an impenetrable sea of cars stands between my brother and me. I must be cursed.

32

The skies ahead of me are darkening with smoke, delicate pieces of ash are hovering in the air. I have my window rolled up, but the smell of smoke from the raging wildfire permeates within the car as helicopters carrying massive buckets of water circle overhead. I can't stay here. I need to move.

Sirens and air horns blare in the distance before half a dozen red and yellow firetrucks caravan down the shoulder along the highway, passing traffic. I put my car in gear and take chase after the last fire engine to the next off-ramp.

I manage to reach the city line before a highway patrol officer stops me. I show her my FBI badge and am granted passage past the police barricades ahead.

The city is under siege. Chaos reigns. People are desperately trying to get away from the inferno. Cops are attempting to manage traffic, but laws and regulations have little worth when people are running for their lives.

The opposite side is moving slowly, full of impatiently honking cars and people yelling. My lane is wide open as I head toward the fire, where fingers of red and orange flames are climbing up the mountain. The temperature is rising. The layer of ash descending on me is thickening. More firetrucks race up behind me. I pull over to let them pass.

I'm stopped by police again. It takes more convincing this time to be granted access to the fire and community ahead.

Forget Lake Elsinore. A colossal wildfire is consuming the city. I send a warning text to Anaya's phone.

She immediately calls, but I don't answer.

Two minutes away from Blake's house, the blazing hillsides are vividly alive with fire. Like a giant red growing amoeba, the flames consume the parched vegetation, chasing wild animals from their homes. A raccoon with three babies is crossing the street in front of me. I stop, mesmerized by the destruction and suffering Mother Nature inflicts on herself and her children.

I see a team of brave firefighters, faces blackened with soot, making a stand against a wall of fire, as tongues of flames try to lap at the houses within reach. My respect for my sister and her job grows exponentially.

I stop the car and continue on foot as the road becomes too hazardous to drive any further. I pass families rushing to pack up their cars, not willing to let go of their memories and valued possessions. Parents are screaming at their kids to stop staring at the fire and get inside the car. Teenagers, standing like zombies, are recording the disaster on their smartphones. Two police officers are chasing a man running with a PlayStation pressed against his chest, which he ultimately discards in a ditch to run faster. The cops catch up to him, push him to the ground, and cuff his hands behind his back.

I have to show my ID to the people in charge of public safety three more times before I reach the house. It's still intact, the wind blowing the fire in the opposite direction. A loud rumbling sound of an aircraft overhead draws my eyes to the sky as a low-flying airplane drops a line of orange fire-retardant along the edge of the residential community.

I don't see a car parked by the house. Either nobody is home or the tenants have parked in the garage. If Blake lives here with Jenna, I assume they've already evacuated the area. I should leave too, but I feel an enormous gravitational pull toward the house. This is where my brother lives, or lived, at one point in his life. I want to touch the walls and feel his presence. People say twins have a special bond. I need to experience it.

I knock on the door.

No answer.

I jump the fence and try the back door.

It's locked.

I peek through windows. I remove screens and pull at each lock until I find an open window. I climb inside and drop into a room that looks to be the guestroom.

I open the drawers. All empty.

I move into the bathroom. Cleaned out.

I walk to the kitchen. The dishwasher is empty, but the cabinets contain a few cups and plates.

The whole house looks to have been prepared for potential buyers' visits.

The garage is the only place I find some personal items stored in bins. I pop a blue top open and delve into the contents. I see a 2003 Temescal Canyon High School yearbook. Blake isn't in it.

I take out a stack of photos. There are mostly pictures of a pretty young girl with strawberry-blonde hair and a young Hispanic male, at least five years her senior. I flip a few photos over. No dates or names are written on the back.

Cheerleading outfits, a baseball glove, DVDs, CDs, shoes, and clothes.

Disappointed, I sit back on my heels, trying to make sense of what I'm seeing here. If this is the home of Jenna Davis, Blake's pen pal from prison eight years ago, and possible girlfriend, then the guy in the photos must be the girl's husband. But if the husband is still in the picture, why would Blake give this address to a handyman to fix the roof?

I go through a few more boxes. No recent photos. All of them are at least a decade old. None of this makes sense.

I keep searching, hoping to uncover an address to another one of Blake's properties because it's obvious he isn't living here.

A police loudspeaker warns citizens to evacuate immediately. It's scary sitting in this dark, dirty garage not knowing if the wind has changed direction or not. The fire could be blowing away from me or about to consume me. It's silly to be risking my life going through this useless junk, but if I don't find a clue, then I'll have no way of finding my brother.

My phone buzzes in my back pocket. It must be a text from Anaya, probably complaining about me not answering her call earlier. I'm reluctant to click on the message. I know I'm probably in trouble—I don't need her to tell me.

My throat is parched, and it's getting increasingly difficult to breathe. I head to the kitchen to drink water from the tap.

I hear the garage door motor. Someone is here.

I freeze with panic. It could be the police responsible for the evacuation, or firefighters. Or Anaya for all I know. Either way, I don't want to get caught for breaking and entering, or for conducting an illegal search without a warrant.

I step behind the refrigerator for cover and wait.

The motor whines again. The garage door is closing. I hear the door open from the garage, then footsteps. A face comes into view. My heart drops into my stomach.

"What the—! What are *you* doing here?" I call out to Ethan, my boyfriend's business partner and lover.

His face goes pale with surprise as he jumps back, slamming his back against the doorframe.

"What the fuck!" he shouts at me. "How did you get here?"

My mouth opens to speak, but the sound doesn't come out. I don't understand what Ethan is doing here.

My phone vibrates again. The sound is loud in the dead silence. Ethan takes a hostile stance, staring at me with dark eyes.

I pull my phone out and read the message from Anaya.

Here's a screenshot of the guy who spat on Meredith's jacket.

I scroll down to the picture and the blood stops in my veins. I'm about to have a heart attack. I can't breathe. It's undoubtedly my close friend, Doug's business partner and lover, who stands beside Meredith, wearing his stupid lumberjack beard and mustache and a furious expression on his face.

I slowly move my eyes to Ethan. I'm trained to mask my emotions, but I fail miserably. He knows that I know.

Ethan drops the bag in his hand to the floor and slowly grins. "Shit! You found out, didn't you? I always knew you were a damn good detective."

"Blake?" I breathe his name, a cold chill running down my spine.

He holds my gaze for a moment, then suddenly switches off the light. I find myself standing in darkness with only a slight red glow from the fire outside, in a strange house, trembling with uncertainty and fearing for my life.

33

I squat down and pull my Glock from its holster. I see a shadow move quickly across the room and disappear behind the breakfast nook. I don't want to shoot my brother, but I may have no choice.

My breathing is raspy, fast, and loud, giving away my position. I feel like a rookie agent.

I squint, waiting for my eyes to adjust to the dimness.

"Blake, I only want to talk," I plead desperately, my voice rising and falling with my rapid heartbeat.

"Don't call me that! Blake died ten years ago."

I aim my weapon in the direction of the angry voice, my hands shaking as I try to frantically focus on my training. I've never been in an officer-involved shooting. I've only pursued criminals online.

I duck-walk toward the door to look for a light switch. "I know what happened to you, Blake. I'm here to help you. Please, I only want to help."

"You don't know shit about me! You women are all the same. You're users. And when we're no longer needed, you chew us up and spit us out. But when we need help? You disappear." He is somewhere behind me. I spin around and nearly lose my balance. I scan the gloomy room for his silhouette. Nothing.

I reach back and flip on the light switch. It doesn't work. Blake must have shut off the breakers to the house. My only hope of getting some light in here is through the blinds. As I inch toward the closest window in the living room, I hear a drawer open and utensils rattle.

My heart is in my throat. I can't believe my twin brother would hurt me, but he's damaged goods, a killer, likely a maniac serial killer who's managed to elude justice for a decade.

I stumble over an ottoman but regain my footing before I fall to the ground. I lean against the wall and rip the blinds down. A faint reddish-orange glow floods the room.

"Why did you come here? Why did you have to ruin everything?"

I can hear him, but he knows where to hide. Panic overcomes me. I switch the aim of my Glock rapidly as the flickering light from the fire that casts images on the walls plays tricks with my mind.

"I came to help you. Please, let's just talk."

"How did you find me?"

The gun is heavy in my hands, and the muscles in my arms start twitching. I don't know how much longer I can keep this up, but I do know that I don't want to die here today. I don't want to kill my brother either. But I must stop him, or at least, slow him down, so I desperately search for a target in the dim room. I fail. Blake's voice seems to be coming from every direction. He's toying with me.

"I retraced your past. I talked to your aunt and our biological father."

"Don't talk about those monsters to me!" he roars. I shudder.

"Okay. Okay. So, what do you want to talk about?"

"I'm not going back to prison."

"I understand. I can get you help. I know what happened to you when you were growing up. You were just a kid. It wasn't your fault. You deserve justice."

"You don't know shit about what happened!" His voice, like a storm, fills the room. "That wasn't me. That was a pathetic, weak, little boy who let those men do whatever they wanted to him. That boy died a long time ago."

"It wasn't your fault."

"It *was* my fault!" he shouts, and I almost drop my gun because it sounds as if he's right behind me, but he isn't.

"The system failed you. You were only a child. You can't blame yourself."

"I could have stolen a knife from the kitchen and killed those motherfuckers. Do you have any idea how helpless it feels to grow up too scared to close your eyes every night because you never know which monster will visit you? I let them do those things to me."

"Your aunt was supposed to protect you, look after you."

"Well, she didn't. My mother let me down too. She gave up on me and on her own life after my father died. I was worth living for, but she was too selfish to see it." His voice is haunting me.

"I know, but . . . depression is a sickness. She didn't give up on you, she was sick."

"I'm tired of listening to women's pathetic excuses for not doing their jobs. Oh, it's so hard to raise a child. Oh, it's so hard to be married. If everything is so fucking hard for you, why don't you kill yourselves and save us the trouble!"

"Is that why you punished all those women, Blake? Because you hate women?"

"Stop calling me Blake!" I feel his breath on the back of my neck, but it's too late for me to react. He has a knife against my throat. "Drop the gun!"

"Alright. Alright—look . . . I'm putting it on the floor right now. But you need to relax, okay? I know you don't want to hurt your sister."

He scoffs. "My sister, huh? My little princess sister who had everything she wanted in life?"

I need to establish trust between us, bring up a memory we share.

"You're my friend, Ethan. You've known me for years. Why didn't you say something?"

"Oh, and tell you what? That I'm your lost little brother who was raped by disgusting fat men with small limp dicks? Do you have any idea how hard it is to have a normal relationship after that? All I think about is what my girlfriend will say when she finds out about my childhood."

"I wouldn't have judged you."

He pushes me against the wall and presses the knife against my chest. "You only just found out who you really are! You just met your real father. You've been living in a perfect little bubble," he sneers through clenched teeth.

"I didn't know. Nobody told me."

He wipes his mouth with the back of his hand and smooths down his overgrown beard. He looks me dead in the eye. "I kissed you, sis. I slept with your boyfriend."

"Why? Were you trying to hurt me?" I whisper.

"Were you trying to hurt me?" he repeats mockingly. "If I wanted to hurt you, I would have. All your education and training wasn't enough to catch me. I knew you were onto me. I drugged you while we were watching fireworks on the fourth, then I searched your laptop. You were the one who found out about my little scheme, but you had no clue it was me."

"I wish it wasn't."

He chuckles, stepping back from me. "But it was me. It is me."

"I can get you help. You can still come out of this okay."

I step toward him. A big mistake. He reads my move as an act of aggression, and jumps at me, tossing me to the ground. He sits on my stomach and pushes the knife against my chest.

"I don't need your help. You are not my little sister. We are *nothing!*"

He's heavy, and I'm struggling to breathe. Tears gather in my eyes from the strain.

"My father is your father. His rapist blood is in my veins too. I won't let him or anything else from my past to ruin me. You can do the same. You have more strength than I do," I say, wheezing.

"Well, aren't you a perfect little sister!" He spits into my face, and his warm saliva trickles down on the bridge of my nose. "I guess you handled life better than I did. Or maybe you never had to experience true pain and humiliation like I did. The feeling of lying there, powerless, unable to move. Well, let's see how you come back from this."

He rips the buttons off my shirt and cuts off my bra.

I wriggle underneath him, trying to break free. He presses the blade of the knife against my throat, and this time, it cuts into my flesh.

"You don't want to do this, Blake. I'm your sister. Your twin sister, dammit. We shared a womb."

"Shut up! Shut the hell up!" He presses his fist against his forehead, then he shakes his head.

I scan the floor for my gun while Blake unfastens his belt and cuts off mine.

"Stop, Ethan! I know you don't want to do this."

He leans close to my face. "You know nothing about me. Or what I want. Or what I do."

As I look into his dark eyes, I realize that my brother died long ago. This man is a shell of a child he might have been once upon a time, reduced to an empty soul. He will rape and kill me. I've come to terms with it. I flex my body and roll my fingers in a ball. My stomach churns and twists, gathering my anger and fear into a source of willpower. I close my eyes and jerk my torso up, slamming my forehead into his nose. I hear a crack, followed by a painful bellowing. Blake touches his face. Blood is already flowing between his fingers and down his face.

"You *bitch*!" he screams and raises the knife in his hand. The fire burning outside reflects off the shiny blade. This is the end. My fingers fumble for the gun, brush against the warm metal. I can touch it, but it's too far for me to get a firm hold.

I feel his warm blood dripping onto my face. I scratch Blake's skin on his arm to get his DNA underneath my nails. I know I'm going to die at the hands of my own brother and this is how I leave evidence for the police to find my killer.

Two bursts of thunder rip through the room. The loud bangs are deafening and my ears start to ring. Blake's eyes are lifeless as he falls on top of me, his weight crushing me. I tuck in my arms, trying to roll him off me.

"Vicky!"

What—?

"Are you okay?" I hear Anaya's voice again, then see her ebony hand pulling off my brother.

Brestler appears next to us with his gun drawn. He kicks the limp body over and onto its back. "Are you hurt?"

"N-no, I don't think s-so," I say in a mere whisper, touching my neck. My fingers return with blood on them. "Just a cut."

Brestler puts his hand on my head. "Good. Very good." Then he looks at Anaya. "Call it in."

Anaya's puppy eyes linger a second longer on me, then she lifts her phone to her ear and makes the call.

* * * * *

Everything has happened so fast, and my mind is still catching up with reality. I feel cold and disoriented like I'm in a dream.

I put two fingers on Blake's neck. No pulse. He's gone. I don't know how to feel about his death. I knew him as a friend, my boyfriend's business partner and his lover.

But he is, or was, my brother—my twin brother. We were both robbed of the truth, but he was the one who ultimately paid the price for it.

Anaya crouches down beside me. "I told you not to come here alone. You could have gotten yourself killed."

I lick my lips, battling against emotions. "It's not fair, you know. Adults can abuse children then leave them broken and beyond repair, and get away with it. Blake's childhood wasn't his fault—he's a victim, too."

"I know you're confused and in shock right now, Vicky, but he had a choice, and he chose wrong. He killed people."

I smooth my hair back and push myself to my feet. "I know he did. But now I see that the devil doesn't walk among us, whispering in our ears. *People* are evil, Anaya, people. We create our own monsters."

The next hour passes in a blur. Flashing blue and red lights bounce off the walls of the house, competing for canvas space with the raging wildfire. The firefighters give us an hour to search the house for evidence before a mandatory evacuation.

Over a dozen sheriff deputies show up to tear apart Blake's house inch by inch. The cadaver dogs find two skeletons in a shallow grave in the backyard by a eucalyptus tree. A male and a female, presumably in their early twenties. I assume they are Jenna Davis and her husband, but we won't know for sure until the autopsy report comes back. Based on the conditions of the decomposed bodies, it may take days or weeks.

In the attic, we find a shrine dedicated to the victims of the Piggyback Serial Killer, my twin brother, Blake Sullivan, also known as Ethan Davis. I never knew Ethan's last name. If I did, I might have solved the mystery faster. But you never know. Everybody is smarter in hindsight.

Seeing all this evidence against him, I now understand why Blake returned to this house on the night of the fire.

As Brestler and Anaya pack up the photos Blake took of his victims and the trophy items he collected from everyone he killed and displayed in a glass vitrine, I count and log forty-seven victims. Mostly women and four men under age thirty. Many names I recognize from our special investigation. We were onto him. If only we had a little more time—

Blake must have been confused about his sexuality, which made him angry and violent. The sexual abuse he was a victim to at an early age is to blame.

As I ponder how unfair life is, a rage burns stronger deep inside me. I want justice for my brother, but I will never get it. I feel for his victims. I do. But it's like a domino effect. One selfish and narcissist woman's actions led to this tragedy. Then one domino after the other fell. If only his aunt had been a decent person—

The wind has changed direction, and despite the tremendous effort by the firefighters, the fire jumped the boundaries of the community. I watch Blake's house be engulfed in flames from the backseat of Brestler's car with a heavy heart.

The chief's call comes in on my cellphone. He congratulates me on solving one of the most prominent murder cases this country has ever seen. He says he sees a bright future for me in the Bureau. I don't feel glorious. How could I after getting my brother killed to solve the case?

I hold my phone in my hand until we reach San Diego, staring at my mother's phone number on the screen. Then with a sudden change of heart, I call Doug instead.

"Hey, there," he answers timidly. "I'm glad you called. I really need to talk to you. To apologize."

"Yeah, let's talk."

"I'm home. I left the convention early. I couldn't stay any longer. I can't seem to pack up my stuff either. I don't want to leave you, Vicky."

I swallow my tears. "I don't think I want you to leave either."

"Do you think there's any way we can work through this? I'm not attracted to men. Really. It was a mistake. I love you. What I did . . . what we did . . . That was stupid."

"Let's not discuss this over the phone. I'm not alone."

"Oh, yeah, okay. Are you going to be home anytime soon?"

"We have a ton of paperwork to fill out at the office, but then I'm heading home."

"Good. I mean, great. I bought a couple of steaks. Do you want to text me when you're ten minutes out, and I'll throw them on the grill?"

"You may want to grab a bottle of something strong too. Tequila? I won't be coming home with good news."

"Look, Vicky, at least let me explain. Please, give me another chance to prove to you how important you are to me."

"It's not about us, Doug. I'll tell you everything when I get home," I promise. I hang up the phone, knowing I will give Doug a second chance.

Because everybody deserves a second chance.
Don't they?

THE END

Titles by A. B. Whelan

14 Days to Die (a psychological thriller)
As Sick as Our Secrets (a psychological thriller)

The Fields of Elysium Saga
(YA Romantic Fantasy)
Fields of Elysium (Book One)
Valley of Darkness (Book Two)
City of Shame (Book Three)
Return to Innocence (Book Four)
Safe and Sound (Novella)

Connect with The Author Online

For early access to new books, giveaways, and more join:
A.B. Whelan's Best Book Friends on Facebook

Goodreads
Author Facebook Page: Author A B Whelan
Instagram: @authorabwhelan
Twitter: @authorabwhelan

Made in the USA
Middletown, DE
30 August 2020